Dear Reader,

I have always taken charge, taken control, taken without asking. And here I am, a successful forty-one-year-old man, the widowed father of a seventeen-year-old, and no one has ever taught me a lesson about taking what isn't mine until now, until I met Nacia Barns on an Atlantic City beach.

The first thing Nacia taught me was that she surrendered to me only with her body, not with her soul. The second was that, even *if* I ask, her heart isn't mine for the taking. So, unless the gamblers roaming the boardwalks and casinos have some luck to spare, I just might lose her....

Jared Ranklin

New Jersey

1. ALABAMA
Full House • Jackie Weger
2. ALASKA
Borrowed Dreams • Debbie Macomber
3. ARIZONA
Call It Destiny • Jayne Ann Krentz
4. ARKANSAS
Another Kind of Love • Mary Lynn Baxter
5. CALIFORNIA
Deceptions • Annette Broadrick
6. COLORADO
Stormwalker • Dallas Schulze
7. CONNECTICUT
Straight from the Heart • Barbara Delinsky
8. DELAWARE
Author's Choice • Elizabeth August
9. FLORIDA
Dream Come True • Ann Major
10. GEORGIA
Way of the Willow • Linda Shaw
11. HAWAII
Tangled Lies • Anne Stuart
12. IDAHO
Rogue's Valley • Kathleen Creighton
13. ILLINOIS
Love by Proxy • Diana Palmer
14. INDIANA
Possibles • Lass Small
15. IOWA
Kiss Yesterday Goodbye • Leigh Michaels
16. KANSAS
A Time To Keep • Curtiss Ann Matlock
17. KENTUCKY
One Pale, Fawn Glove • Linda Shaw
18. LOUISIANA
Bayou Midnight • Emilie Richards
19. MAINE
Rocky Road • Anne Stuart
20. MARYLAND
The Love Thing • Dixie Browning
21. MASSACHUSETTS
Pros and Cons • Bethany Campbell
22. MICHIGAN
To Tame a Wolf • Anne McAllister
23. MINNESOTA
Winter Lady • Janet Joyce
24. MISSISSIPPI
After the Storm • Rebecca Flanders
25. MISSOURI
Choices • Annette Broadrick

26. MONTANA
Part of the Bargain • Linda Lael Miller
27. NEBRASKA
Secrets of Tyrone • Regan Forest
28. NEVADA
Nobody's Baby • Barbara Bretton
29. NEW HAMPSHIRE
Natural Attraction • Marisa Carroll
30. NEW JERSEY
Moments Harsh, Moments Gentle • Joan Hohl
31. NEW MEXICO
Within Reach • Marilyn Pappano
32. NEW YORK
In Good Faith • Judith McWilliams
33. NORTH CAROLINA
The Security Man • Dixie Browning
34. NORTH DAKOTA
A Class Act • Kathleen Eagle
35. OHIO
Too Near the Fire • Lindsay McKenna
36. OKLAHOMA
A Time and a Season • Curtiss Ann Matlock
37. OREGON
Uneasy Alliance • Jayne Ann Krentz
38. PENNSYLVANIA
The Wrong Man • Ann Major
39. RHODE ISLAND
The Bargain • Patricia Coughlin
40. SOUTH CAROLINA
The Last Frontier • Rebecca Flanders
41. SOUTH DAKOTA
For Old Times' Sake • Kathleen Eagle
42. TENNESSEE
To Love a Dreamer • Ruth Langan
43. TEXAS
For the Love of Mike • Candace Schuler
44. UTAH
To Tame the Hunter • Stephanie James
45. VERMONT
Finders Keepers • Carla Neggers
46. VIRGINIA
The Devlin Dare • Cathy Gillen Thacker
47. WASHINGTON
The Waiting Game • Jayne Ann Krentz
48. WEST VIRGINIA
All in the Family • Heather Graham Pozzessere
49. WISCONSIN
Starstruck • Anne McAllister
50. WYOMING
Special Touches • Sharon Brondos

JOAN HOHL
Moments Harsh,
Moments Gentle

New Jersey

Published by Silhouette Books New York

America's Publisher of Contemporary Romance

SILHOUETTE BOOKS
300 East 42nd St., New York, N.Y. 10017

MOMENTS HARSH, MOMENTS GENTLE

Copyright © 1984 by Joan Hohl

ISBN: 0-373-45180-6

Published Silhouette Books 1984, 1993

All the characters in this book have no existence outside the
imagination of the author and have no relation whatsoever to
anyone bearing the same name or names. They are not even
distantly inspired by any individual known or unknown to the
author, and all incidents are pure invention.

Printed in the U.S.A.

Chapter 1

The door closed with a gentle click, followed by a soft groan of relief.

"Hi, Mom. You look kinda wilted. Rough day?"

The full-bodied woman slumping against the door straightened to her normal height of five feet, seven and one-half inches.

"Yes." Nacia's naturally low voice was raspy with fatigue. Pushing away from the door, she walked into the living room, her eyes filled with amusement at the sight of her nearly upside-down daughter, Tracy. The fourteen-year-old grinned as she slowly lowered her legs from their high hatha-yoga shoulder stand position. "Is there coffee?" Nacia asked, skirting the now prone, relaxed, slender form of the youngster, and heading for the kitchen.

"Mmmhmmm, fresh pot," Tracy intoned between deep breaths.

Smiling indulgently, Nacia entered the apartment's small compact kitchen. Dropping her handbag and briefcase onto the first chair she passed, she walked to the short counter top between the sink and stove, on which rested the plastic and glass coffeemaker. After plucking an earthenware mug from the cabinet above the counter, she filled it with the rich, dark brew, sniffing its aromatic steam appreciatively.

"I thought all executives made a beeline for the martini pitcher the minute they got home from work," Tracy drawled teasingly as she strolled into the room.

Nacia took a reviving sip of the hot liquid before replying. "I don't know about other executives, but this particular one is addicted to caffeine." A smile banished the lines of weariness from her face. "And how was your day, honey?"

"Fair to middlin'," Tracy said, repeating one of her grandfather's stock responses. "I zapped through the joint with a dust rag and the vacuum, then I went down to the pool with Terri for a couple of hours."

Nacia's smile was again indulgent as she studied her daughter's animated, heart-shaped face. For possibly the thousandth time, she marveled that she had produced this small, delicately boned creature that, from day one, had shown promise of real beauty.

Nacia was no beauty; nor was she small or in any way delicate in appearance. Quite the contrary. From the time she was old enough to notice such things, she had realized, oftentimes painfully, that she was bigger than other girls her age. Not only did she stand higher, she usually stood wider.

Nacia loved to eat. Most particularly, she loved to eat chocolate, and as a child, she had. A lot. By the time she was fifteen, she had grown to her full height. That summer she attained the weight of one hundred and sixty-two pounds. That same summer she started her first diet. She had been dieting on and off ever since.

Being neither blind nor stupid, Nacia knew she was not unattractive. The chocolate notwithstanding, she had a complexion that had always been the envy of her friends—all of whom seemed to break out in spots at the mention of the word "candy." If not spectacular, her features were even and in the right place. Her lips were full and well shaped, and when parted, revealed a set of even white teeth. Nacia admitted—at least to herself—that on more than one occasion she had smile-dazzled her way out of a tight or uncomfortable situation.

Now, at thirty-five, Nacia still had to watch her diet for, as she liked to say, everything she ate went directly to her hips. She sighed over every bypassed dessert, but for the last several years she had managed to keep her weight at a steady one hundred and thirty pounds.

"What would you like for dinner?" Tracy's question jolted Nacia out of her reverie.

"A Milky Way bar."

"Frozen or gooey?" Tracy, fully aware of her mother's sweet tooth, grinned.

"Any way I can get it." Nacia grinned back.

"Will you settle for one of my special chicken salads with low-cal dressing?"

Nacia pretended to give her daughter's suggestion serious consideration. Tilting her head, she ran her solemn, brown-eyed gaze over her pert-faced off-spring. "Does it have white grapes in it?"

"Certainly!" Tracy exclaimed in an affronted tone.

"Walnuts?"

"But of course!" Tracy managed a fair French accent.

"Sold." Nacia waved her hand in the direction of the refrigerator. "You wouldn't happen to have some kind of low-cal dessert, would you?" she asked hopefully.

Laughing softly, Tracy shook her head in wonder. "I don't know," she laughed, "but sometimes I get this feeling we have our roles confused." Opening the refrigerator door, she reached inside and withdrew a luscious-looking dessert. "I found the recipe for this in a magazine. I hope it's as good as it looks."

"It *looks* fattening." Nacia frowned, visibly eating the concoction with her eyes. "What is in that?"

"All good stuff," Tracy vowed. "Fresh fruit, low-cal cream cheese, skim milk, and low-cal sweetener." She grinned at the look of longing on her mother's face. "You're gonna love it."

"Very likely," Nacia drawled, a rueful smile curving her lips.

Having had her usual lunch of plain yogurt and black coffee, Nacia savored every forkful of her cool salad, and every spoonful of the deceptively rich-looking dessert. Tracy, as usual, chattered nonstop throughout the meal, recounting the typical teenage conversation that had ensued during her hours spent at the pool that was part of the apartment complex. Smiling, nodding, or murmuring a reply where necessary, Nacia felt the tensions of her workday ease out of her until, near the end of the meal, they all came rushing back tenfold when Tracy casually mentioned Nacia's former husband.

"Dad called today."

"And?" Nacia asked tightly.

"He said he'll pick me up right after dinner tomorrow evening." Tracy paused to wet her lips, then rushed on, "You don't mind my going with them, do you?" By "them" Tracy was referring to her father, his second wife, and their six-year-old twin daughters.

"Would it matter if I did?" Nacia was instantly sorry, both for her bitter tone and the actual words. "I'm sorry, honey," she apologized at once, feeling sick at the stricken expression on her daughter's face. "But I can't pretend. I *do* mind. I mind very much, but I also understand." Sighing softly, she caught Tracy's hand with her own much bigger one and squeezed gently. "I'm afraid I've become very possessive of you." This time her sigh was deeper, heartfelt. "I suppose he has as much right to you as I do." Forcing a smile, she gave Tracy's hand another squeeze before releasing it. "Go, and have a good time—although how anyone can have a good time in Florida in midsummer is beyond me. The heat will be brutal."

"I love the heat, and you know it!" Tracy exclaimed, then added softly, "So does Dad." She hesitated, then blurted, "Why do you always call him *he? He* has a name, you know."

"Oh, yes, I do know." Nacia bit her lip against the encroaching sound of renewed bitterness. "Okay." She smiled ruefully. "Your father, Clayton Barns, has every right to spend part of the summer with you, but, dammit, why does it have to be while I'm on vacation?''

"Dad didn't know you'd be on vacation at the same time as he was!" Tracy protested her father's innocence. "It just worked out that way."

I'll bet! Nacia managed to keep the snort of disbelief to herself. Be fair, her conscience scolded. Maybe, just maybe, he really hadn't known. Even if he had, it made no difference now. Tracy was going with him, and Nacia hated the very idea! Actually, she hated the very idea of Clay Barns simply because she hated *him*. Giving herself a mental shake, she rose and began clearing the table. "Are you all packed and ready to go?" Nacia paused in the act of squirting detergent into the sink and raised a finely arched eyebrow at the girl.

"Yes." Tracy nodded, smiling tentatively. "Except for the last-minute stuff, and—" her smile grew impish "—I have to hit you up for some money."

"I'm way ahead of you." Nacia returned the smile. "I stopped by the bank at lunchtime and bought you some traveler's checks."

"To the tune of how much?" Tracy rubbed her hands with mock greed.

"Enough." This time Nacia allowed herself the snort. She named a figure that brought a gleam to Tracy's eyes and a squeal to her lips. Two slim arms circled her neck, and Nacia had to swallow against the lump in her throat as she was rewarded with a fierce hug and a smacking kiss.

"You're super!" Tracy exclaimed fervently. "The best mother in the entire world. Everyone says so."

"Who's everyone?" Nacia laughed, arching her brow skeptically.

"All my friends," Tracy averred. "No kidding, even the boys think you're great! They all want you to adopt them."

"Because I indulge you," Nacia teased. "Outrageously."

"Yeah," Tracy admitted with calm unconcern. "But then, I'm a pretty neat kid, too."

Nacia nodded seriously at her daughter's bland statement. In truth, Tracy was more than a pretty neat kid, she was one terrific kid! There were moments, like now, when Nacia wondered at how she had managed single-handedly to raise such a delightfully normal, happy child. She could count on one hand the instances when Tracy had given her uneasy moments. Perhaps, Nacia mused, Tracy was her compensation for the hours of unease she had suffered with her father. Averting her face, Nacia grimaced and dismissed all thought of her former husband.

"What are you going to do while I'm in Florida?" Tracy's question brought a smile to Nacia's face. With the conceit of the very young, Tracy could not imagine her mother being able to enjoy herself on her own for two whole weeks.

"I don't know." Nacia shrugged. "Catch up on my sleep, and on some of the books I've been wanting to read." Casting a critical glance around the now-gleaming kitchen, she nodded in satisfaction. "Maybe," she went on, as they walked out of the kitchen, "I'll take a run down to Atlantic City and throw away some of my hard-earned money."

"All by yourself!" Tracy stopped in her tracks to stare at her in shocked disbelief.

"I'm a big girl now, in case you hadn't noticed," Nacia chided teasingly. "Why shouldn't I go by myself?"

"Well, you know," Tracy moaned. "A woman alone, in a place like that!"

"A place like that!" Nacia couldn't help herself; she burst out laughing. "Whatever are you talking about? Do you have any idea of how many little old ladies go to a place like that? Atlantic City is a resort, for heaven's sake."

Tracy's face revealed her dissatisfaction. "But you're not a little old lady, you are a very—in my friend Steve's words—foxy lady. And there are all types of men on the prowl down there for foxy ladies."

Nacia could say nothing for several seconds. She had never had the vaguest idea that the boys Tracy traveled around with thought her attractive, let alone foxy! "I hate to be the one to break the news to you, my love, but there are all kinds of men everywhere constantly on the prowl for ladies—foxy or otherwise." Her laughter subsided to an understanding smile. "You needn't worry about me," she said soothingly. "As practice really does make perfect, I have a positive talent for discouraging men. So you just go south with an easy mind. I'll be perfectly all right." Nacia was to remember her boastful words with chagrin not too many days later.

Friday was one of those days that everyone has, and nobody needs. Maybe it was the fact that Nacia was preoccupied with thoughts of Tracy's imminent departure. Or, perhaps it was the fact that the air-conditioning system in the office could not keep up with the humidity. Whatever it was, from the minute she entered her office until the minute she escaped, everything that could go wrong, did. Sales invoices were mislaid. Several files that Nacia needed seemed to have grown legs and taken a stroll. Her secretary, who was normally a superefficient woman, missed some very important points at a very important sales meeting. By the time Nacia pushed her chair away from her desk and cried quits, she was hot, tired, irritable, and feeling just about nasty enough to face Clayton Barns.

Of course, the traffic around Philadelphia was a congested mess. For possibly the hundredth time Nacia asked herself why the firm she worked for, Uniforms Inc., still maintained offices in the city; didn't management know that everyone else had relocated in the suburbs? Thank heaven her car's air-conditioning was performing efficiently. When, finally, she drove the three-year-old Buick Regal down the ramp to the apartment's underground parking lot, she was no longer hot but, if possible, she was even more irritable. Bring on the former mate! she told herself grimly.

Clay arrived on schedule right after dinner. Composing her features into a mask of cool disdain, Nacia slowly followed her galloping daughter into the living room, fighting back a feeling of dismay at Tracy's eagerness.

"Hi, Dad." Tracy's exuberant greeting caused Nacia a twinge of pain. "I'm all packed and ready to go. All I have to do is make a last-minute visit to the bathroom."

"Take your time, Trace." The smile that curved Clay's full lips twisted grimly as he added, "I'm sure your mother has a list of dos and don'ts to lay on me." At the worried expression that washed over Tracy's face, he nudged her. "Go do your thing, honey. I fully intend to comply with every one of your mother's dictates." Reassured, Tracy dashed out of the room.

During this exchange Nacia had availed herself of the opportunity to study the man she had so foolishly married right out of high school, and divorced less than three years later.

In looks, Clay was little changed, except for the lines of maturity that scored his little-boy, good-looking face, and the specks of gray that dusted his light brown hair. His slightly above average height now supported some twenty-odd more pounds, lending his frame a burly appearance. If Tracy's reports could be believed, the major change in Clay was in his temperament. Nacia had listened to Tracy's accounts of her father's forbearance with a bland expression and a disbelieving mind. *She* had every reason to know better. Now, as he turned his sky-blue eyes to her, Nacia took extreme pleasure in speaking her mind.

"Actually," she informed him coolly, "I have only one last-minute instruction for you." His pale eyebrows arched. "Take care of her," she said icily.

Annoyance flashed briefly across Clay's features and was quickly replaced by a look of defeat. "You just can't bring yourself not to hate me, can you, Nac?"

"I haven't tried," she retorted honestly. "But, whether I hate you or not has nothing to do with it.

You take care of *my* daughter.'' She had used the singular possessive deliberately.

"She is *my* daughter too, you sharp-tongued shrew!" Realizing that his response was what she had expected, Clay flushed a deep red. "You still feel the need to punish me, don't you?" Not bothering to wait for an answer, he went on evenly, "I would no more let anything happen to Tracy than I would to the twins. Hard as it may be for you to believe, I do love her."

"What I find hard to believe, Clayton, is that it took you almost ten years to discover your so-called love." Nacia had again deliberately baited him, this time by using his full name, which she knew he hated. He's right in one thing, she decided in amusement. I am a shrew.

"Dammit, Nacia!" Clay exploded, thereby increasing her amusement. "I stayed away because I knew you wanted me to, not because I didn't love my daughter." Catching her expression, he narrowed his eyes. "I'm damned if I understand what makes you tick," he sighed. "It's over. It has been over for a long time. Why the hell can't you let it go?"

Nacia's smile was more of a sneer. "You'd love that, wouldn't you?" She shook her head in dismissal. "One word you said explains why I can't let it go. Hell. You put me through pure, unadulterated hell. I don't *ever* want to forget it."

"So you'll spend the rest of your life hating the whole world?"

"No, not the whole world," Nacia corrected him mildly. "Only the males that populate it."

A pitying expression changed Clay's angry, flushed face. "I feel sorry for you, Nacia." His eyes examined her briefly. "You're an attractive woman and, if Tracy can be believed, a terrific mother. You should have remarried years ago and had more babies, instead of clawing your way up the corporate ladder."

"Your concern touches me deeply," Nacia drawled. "You'll have to excuse me if I think it's just a mite too late in coming." Suddenly tired of sticking knives into him, she turned away. "I don't want anything from you, most especially your advice. Go to Florida, have a good time, but—" she paused to emphasize her demand "—bring Tracy back in exactly two weeks."

"You have my word," Clay promised earnestly.

Nacia couldn't resist one last shot. "You have no idea how much having your word relieves my mind."

Clay had obviously had it. "Go to hell, Nacia," he spat.

"I've been." Turning completely, she walked away from him.

Jared Ranklin strolled through the thinning crowd in a brightly lighted, ornately decorated Atlantic City casino. His face expressionless, his disinterested eyes shifting restlessly, he observed the weariness dragging at the pale countenances around him, wondering why, if they were so very tired, they simply didn't pack it in and go home—or to whatever motel or hotel they were staying in—and drop unconscious onto a bed.

Why don't you take your own advice? he asked himself. The question sent a ghost of a grin skittering over his compressed lips. Very probably, because I'm searching, just like they are—if not for the same thing.

The answer startled Jared to a full stop. Searching? For what?

You know what, he told himself. Something to fill the hole that you feel inside. It was not a consciously defined thought, the recognition of that yawning hole. Until that instant, he had not taken the time to acknowledge the need for any kind of "something." He didn't particularly relish the intrusive thought at this time and place, either.

Follow your own advice, Ranklin. Physically moving again, Jared mentally backed away from examining the cause of the emptiness in his life. Make tracks for the bed you've hired, and seek oblivion there.

"Jared?"

Intent on escaping, Jared did not hear the first time his name was called out.

"Jared!"

Head snapping up, Jared pivoted in the direction of the familiar voice.

The call had come from a rotund man standing near a blackjack table a few feet to Jared's right. A grin relieved the tightness of his lips at the sight of the man's smiling round face. Four of Jared's long-legged strides were all that were required to bring him within hand-grasping closeness. The round man was first to speak.

"How the hell are you?" The strength in the pudgy hand that clasped his might have surprised anyone but Jared; he knew the mettle of his friend.

"In comparison to whom?" Jared's retort was a familiar one, eliciting a chuckle from the man's barrel chest. "Who opened the cage door and let you out, Frank?"

"My other half." Frank's chuckle blossomed into a deep, full-bodied laugh. "She's around here somewhere, probably losing most of my money."

"Are you beginning?" Jared tilted his head at the table behind Frank. "Or quitting?"

"Quitting." Frank's grimace told the story of frustration. "I've lost my quota for the night."

Jared's grin spread. "Quota?" He knew the answer, but he wanted to hear Frank admit it.

"Wise guy." Frank grinned back. "You know who holds the purse strings in this outfit. Deb's tighter than the lid on a mason jar."

"I always did maintain that Deb was one clever lady." Jared raised a dark eyebrow. "You blew the roll?"

"Of course." Frank shrugged. "I never could win at blackjack." A smile of contentment curved his full lips. "But I prove the adage: Unlucky at cards, lucky in love."

"Just so you know it." Though Jared's tone was teasing, light, his expression was serious. He, himself, was very lucky at cards. The conversation was leading right back to the "something" he had been attempting to walk away from when Frank had called to him. Again he avoided identifying the cause of his discontent.

"Come along, friend." Jared's tone offered exaggerated consolation. "I'll buy you a beer to cry into."

"I don't drink beer." Frank grinned happily as he attempted to match his short stride to Jared's much longer, loping gait.

"I know." Jared's easy laughter drew smiles from the weary-faced gamblers closest to him. His laughter always drew smiles, even from unwilling hearers. Frank was not one of the unwilling; his own laughter, reinforcing Jared's, said a lot about their friendship.

Relaxing in padded chairs at a minuscule table in the small lounge on the fringes of the casino, sipping slowly at their drinks, the two men caught up on what had been happening in their lives since their last meeting.

"How's the project coming?" Frank asked innocently.

"Project?" Jared drawled disdainfully.

"Picky, picky." Frank grinned unrepentedly. "Okay, how's the development progressing?"

"On schedule."

Frank nearly choked on his drink. A bark of laughter burst from his throat at Jared's blandly offered assertion, even though it was so very typical of his friend; he could not remember ever seeing Jared unsure of anything, especially his work.

"How do you do it?" Frank asked seriously. "I mean, with all the screwups and delays that have become part of life today, how do you always manage to finish on schedule?"

Jared took a long, slow swallow of his drink before answering mockingly, "I scream a lot."

"Bull." Frank's inelegantly snorted reply was met by an exaggerated gasp from behind his chair.

"Frank Evens! How many times have I asked you not to talk like that?" Deborah Evens stepped around the chair to fix a disapproving frown on her husband. At the chuckle that escaped Jared's smiling lips, Deborah shifted her accusing gaze to her long-time friend. "You're as bad as he is, you know that?"

"Sure." Jared's smile softened. "How have you been, Deb?" It was not just a polite question; Jared really wanted to know. Deborah had had some health problems a few months back, and he was concerned for her well-being.

"I'm fine now, Jared." Deborah smiled reassuringly as he produced and held a chair for her. "Thanks to roly-poly there." A nod indicated Frank.

"Roly-poly!" Frank protested indignantly. "Look who's talking!"

Settling her well-padded form more comfortably into her chair, Deborah favored her husband with a complacent smile. "Yes, but *I* have an excuse. My physician assured me it was not unusual to gain weight after surgery."

Sitting back, totally relaxed, Jared soaked up their banter like a dry sponge. He had liked these people the first time he'd met them, when they had come to see and subsequently buy a house in one of his developments almost ten years ago. At that moment, he knew the closest he'd come to acknowledging the emptiness inside was to admit it contained a sort of envy of what Frank and Deborah had together. He knew he'd have to face the truth soon, but not now, and certainly not here!

The reckoning came after their impromptu party had broken up, somewhere around three-thirty in the morning. After agreeing to meet for a late breakfast, they went their separate ways— Frank and Deborah to their room in the hotel, and Jared to the tiny motel room he'd checked into on arrival. In his words, the room was, "So small I have to step outside to change my mind."

Lying on a bed that was not quite long enough, Jared sighed with a longing he had not felt since the months following his wife's sudden, shocking death. Damned if he wasn't, in a word, lonesome! A crooked grin slashed his face. Not for any lack of willing females, he admitted with unconceited honesty. There were several women he could name, without taxing his tired mind, who had made it blatantly obvious just how willing they were.

A nebulous form with an unknown face floated tantalizingly into his head, quickening his tired body into vibrant, aching arousal.

"You are completely nuts, Ranklin," he said aloud.

Enduring, almost enjoying the pain of need, Jared spoke the words in a solemn, quiet tone. Was it mildly insane to crave a woman you had never met? Possibly, he thought. But what the hell, everyone had their weak moments.

Sleep was slow in coming, and short in duration. The wake-up call came, as requested, at exactly nine-thirty, rousing him out of a pleasant dream. Stretching, yawning, and grumbling all the way, he dressed in jeans and a pale blue pullover, then grabbed a cab to the hotel where the Evenses were already ensconced at a table in the restaurant.

"Good morning," Jared began as he slid onto the chair opposite Frank.

"Good morning," Deborah returned, sleepily.

"Sez you," Frank growled. "Will somebody tell me whose idea this was?"

"Yours." Jared and Deborah spoke in unison.

"Oh." Frank grinned sheepishly. "Do you remember why?"

"Oh, Frank, really!" Deborah expelled a long-suffering sigh.

"I think you said something about wanting to get an early start in the oven." Jared supplied the answer.

"Huh?"

"The beach, Frank." Jared nudged his memory. "You said you wanted to hit the sand and start baking before the sun got too high."

"I said that?" Frank groaned. "It's July, for heaven's sake. The sun's already too hot when it sneaks over the horizon!" He cast a dour look at his wife. "How many drinks did I have, anyway?"

"At least three too many." Even though she frowned, Deborah's tone was lightly teasing. "Now, shut up and eat your breakfast."

The meal completed, they parted company, Deborah to go back to bed, the men to go to Jared's motel. As Jared had been only half-awake, he'd forgotten to put on his swim trunks.

"Might as well hit the beach down here," Frank suggested. "It'll probably be less crowded than it is closer to the hotels."

"Wherever," Jared said, shrugging his shoulders. It made no difference to him.

High on the list of Nacia's aversions was getting up early in the morning, yet on the morning after Tracy's departure, her eyes sprang open at first light. The quiet of the apartment should not have seemed unusual as Tracy never disturbed her mother before eleven on any Saturday morning. On this Saturday morning though, the quiet was positively cloying. Two weeks. Two whole weeks! How was she going to fill the hours? Nacia asked herself as she lay listening to the hum of the window air conditioner. When no answer presented itself, she pushed back the dark green-and-white striped sheet and sat up on the edge of the bed, only to stare blankly at the pale green-and-white wallpaper on the opposite wall.

You're a fool, she admonished herself wryly. How many times did you think longingly of a few days all to yourself during the first couple of years of Tracy's life? A sad smile curved her lips as her own mother's admonition whispered through her mind: Be careful what you wish for, Nacia, for you just might get it. Now Nacia was experiencing the truth of her mother's warning.

Nacia's smile turned bitter as she remembered that she had also wished for one Clayton Barns. Thinking his name brought back their confrontation of the evening before, and rushing behind that memory came a flood of other, older ones.

Clay had first come to her notice when the group of boys he hung out with joined the group of girls she was with at a high school basketball game. She could hardly not have noticed him; he had given her a light punch on the arm to get her attention.

"What are you doing after the game?" he'd asked, grinning like an idiot as he watched her rub her arm.

"I don't know," Nacia had answered with forced unconcern, her hand coming to a stop as she gazed into his laughing blue eyes. "Why?" There was no way she could disguise the hopeful note in her voice. Thinking he was the best-looking guy she'd seen in months, Nacia held her breath and prayed his answer was the one she was hoping to hear.

"We're going to Burger-Haven." He indicated the boys he was with with a tilt of his head. "Why don't you stop by?"

She had stopped by, and that was the start of a relationship that was to last four years—four long, pain-filled, humiliating years.

They had both been seniors that year, and the September following graduation she had married him, willfully ignoring her parents' disapproval. Less than six months after their rather lavish wedding, Nacia faced the realization that she should have heeded her parents' advice. They had both been too young, too emotionally immature, and poles apart in their ideas of what marriage was all about. Clay hadn't wanted a wife; he'd wanted a slave. At the time Nacia wasn't sure what she wanted, but she *did* know it wasn't a master.

During the first few weeks they merely argued—often. By the third month they were screaming at each other. Two days shy of their six-month anniversary Clay struck her for the first time—and it was not to be the last.

To Nacia, it seemed that nothing she did was right. If she so much as gave a passing glance to another male, Clay flew into a rage, accusing her of all kinds of wrongdoings. He resented the time, however brief, that she spent with her girlfriends, while he claimed his male right to frequent nights out with the boys. He grimaced at her taste in clothes, and groaned at her taste in home decor. Her first attempts at cooking earned her nothing but an unfair comparison to his mother's culinary skill. But by far the biggest bone of contention between them was her job. She loved it. He hated it.

Nacia had considered herself very fortunate to secure the position of secretary to the assistant sales manager of Uniforms Inc. two weeks before graduation. Within a month of beginning her job, Nacia came to the conclusion that she had found a home away from home. She loved learning about the business as a whole, but most especially she loved the sales end of it. At the beginning she made attempts to discuss her job with Clay, but he became sullen and uncommunicative, and finally, hurt and confused, she gave up in defeat.

They had been married ten months when Nacia became pregnant. She was not surprised, since Clay had forbidden any kind of protection from the first night. She *was* disappointed because she felt they were both too young and their relationship too tenuous to take on the responsibility of a child. Clay, on the other hand, was delighted. At first Nacia had foolishly thought he was overjoyed at the prospect of becoming a father, and she had gazed at him in tenderness. She was swiftly disabused of that notion.

"With a kid to take care of you'll have to quit that damned job and stay at home, where you belong." Clay had not even tried to disguise the malicious tone in his voice. At that time, home was a tiny three-room apartment barely big enough to turn around in. The mere idea of spending every waking minute in the confines of their cramped flat made Nacia feel claustrophobic.

For Nacia, the end came during the third month of her pregnancy. They had been at a party given by her boss, and as Clay had complained bitterly about having to attend in the first place, and had imbibed too much in the short time they were there, he was in a nasty mood when they got home.

"You hand in your notice on Monday morning," he'd ordered the moment the door closed behind them.

"But why?" Nacia cried. "The doctor said I could work until—"

"You'll give notice Monday," Clay snarled. "I saw him, hanging all over you, touching you."

"Who?" Confused by his charge, Nacia stared at him wide-eyed.

"Your boss, that's who. That paragon of business you keep raving on and on about." By then, Clay was shouting, his face mottled with angry color. "What the hell's going on between you two?"

Stunned, Nacia stared at him mutely. Her boss, Jim Hicks, had never, ever made any kind of overt move toward her. Finally finding her voice, Nacia laughed, if somewhat nervously. "Clay, you have got to be kidding. Jim didn't show me any more atten—"

"I'm not blind, Nac. And I'm not dumb." Clay shouted over her protest. "Has he had you?"

"No!" Nacia gasped, shocked and sickened by both his tone and his question. "Clay, you can't believe that I'd—"

"I believe my own eyes," he again interrupted. "And my eyes saw you give him the come-on." Taking a step toward her, he lifted his hand and drew it back.

It was at that moment that the love, or infatuation, or whatever it was that Nacia had felt for him, curled up and died. Something—very likely the expression of horror on her face—stayed his hand in midswing.

"You can be damned glad you're pregnant," he stormed, "because if you weren't, I'd slap you senseless."

The absolute final straw fell when, after they were in bed, his hand slid insinuatingly over her abdomen. "This kid better look like me or you're in big trouble," he warned before he pulled her against him with a rough tug.

For the first time since their wedding night, his seeking hand evoked no excitement, his probing fingers roused not a single flutter in her pulse rate. Lying passive, unmoved by his obvious urgency, she shuddered when his fingers inflicted pain and he growled, "Get with it, girl."

Nacia faked it. That night and every night thereafter she faked her response. He knew it, of course, and the knowing made him brutish in his approach to her. By the time she had left him, three months after Tracy's birth, Nacia's entire being was consumed with disgust and hate, not only for Clay, but for the male of the species in general and the sex act in particular. Merely thinking about it filled her with revulsion.

The divorce had been a nightmare of embarrassment and humiliation. Although Nacia did not have to lie about Clay's less than gentle treatment of her, the actual recounting of it before a judge killed the last bit of youthful eagerness inside her. When it was over and the divorce granted, she hated Clay even more.

Fortunately, Jim Hicks hired her again, and in the intervening years Nacia had steadily, forcefully and coldly worked her way up in the company until she held the title of sales manager, having been promoted to that post at Jim Hicks's retirement three years before.

The early morning sunlight, glaring into her eyes through the bedroom window, brought Nacia back to the here and now. Lips twisting in self-derision, she stood up, tugged her thigh-length nightie over her head, then, shivering in the air-conditioned room, hurried into her bathroom for a wake-up shower.

Twenty minutes later, wrapped in a terry robe, Nacia sat at her dressing table, blow-drying long strands of chestnut hair that had been turned onto a round brush. Tracy favored Clay's side of the family. Clay's mother was small and fragile looking, and still beautiful and youthful in appearance at fifty-seven. Tracy was a near mirror image of her paternal grandmother, except for her hair, which was the same silky texture and shining chestnut color as Nacia's. It was also the same length, so that from the back, the two heads of shoulder-length brown hair were identical.

So, Nacia silently asked her pale image, what are you going to do—sit around and mope, or go catch some sun? Opting for sun, she placed the blow-dryer and brush on the gleaming dresser surface and walked to her closet to retrieve her scarlet suitcase and matching flight bag.

Less than an hour later she tossed both the cases into the trunk of her car, slid behind the wheel and drove away from the apartment complex without a backward glance. Perhaps, she mused whimsically, instead of throwing away some of her hard-earned money, as she'd teasingly said to Tracy, she'd get lucky and win some easy money. Stranger things had happened.

Atlantic City on a hot Saturday morning in July was enough to send any driver's blood pressure soaring. The streets were jammed with an unending line of tour buses, family cars, trucks, limousines, vans and jitneys. And Nacia found herself right in the middle of the cacophonous mass.

Due to her daily dose of congested traffic, Nacia's blood pressure maintained a normal level; but her spirit took a nose dive. Why had she rushed to the beach? In the first place, it was totally out of character. In the second place, she had nowhere to stay!

Patiently waiting for a light to change from red to green, Nacia sighed in recognition of her folly. A wry smile touched her lips as she acknowledged the very real possibility that she would have to spend the night in a room many miles outside the city.

As it turned out, she got lucky. Deciding to follow some oft-repeated advice, she parked the car, found a phone booth, and let her fingers do the walking. Nacia had forgotten how many coins she'd contributed to the phone company when she dialed the number of a motel on Ventnor that, from the address listed in the directory, she judged to be situated near the southernmost end of the famous boardwalk.

On her first try the line was busy. After disconnecting, she counted to fifty and dialed again; eureka!

"Yes, we do," the pleasant-voiced desk clerk replied in answer to her less than hopeful query about accommodations. "As a matter of fact, I had a cancellation just moments ago. I could let you have the room for a full week."

"Sold!" Nacia laughed in sheer relief. "Hang on to that room for me. My name is Nacia Barns, and I will be in your office as fast as the traffic will allow."

Some thirty-odd minutes later, Nacia let herself into a room on the second level of the trilevel, ultramodern motel complex, her checking account balance several hundred dollars less than it had been mere moments ago.

Depositing her large case on the luggage rack and her flight bag on the bed, Nacia ran an appreciative glance over the tastefully decorated room. The walls and ceiling were starkly white, a perfect foil for the rich brown of the plush carpeting and the antique gold of the spread that adorned the queen-size bed.

Over the years, as Nacia had risen through the ranks of the sales department of Uniforms Inc., she had had to attend numerous sales meetings and conferences all over the country. And she had spent more nights than she cared to remember in motel and hotel rooms, many of which were less than spectacular. This room, she decided upon completion of her perusal, was not only elegant, it was invitingly comfortable. Satisfied with her surroundings, she hummed a popular tune softly as she unpacked her cases.

The settling-in process completed, Nacia's thoughts, never far from food anyway, turned to the pressing need for lunch.

In her eagerness to escape her empty apartment and equally empty thoughts, Nacia had gulped two cups of coffee and called them breakfast. Now, over four hours later, her stomach was beginning to feel like a yawning chasm.

After exchanging her denim wraparound skirt and gauze pullover for a peacock-blue maillot and matching ankle-length beach caftan, she made her way to the motel coffee shop, her flat leather slip-ons gently slapping the concrete walkway.

Forty-five minutes later, fortified by a feta cheese omelet, Nacia sipped the last of her iced tea contentedly. After extracting some bills from her wallet, she double-checked her canvas carryall to be sure she had what she needed for the beach. Stuffing the wallet into the very bottom of the bag, she headed for the sand, which was a relatively short distance away as the motel was located at the very fringes of the beach.

Looking down to avoid treading on the supine bodies that literally covered the sand, Nacia came to an abrupt halt, her head snapping up at the sound of her name.

"Hey, Nacia, over here." Following the direction of the voice, Nacia homed in on the rotund figure of Frank Evens, a regional salesman for Uniforms Inc. Frank's arm curled in a beckoning wave, and with a sigh, she stepped carefully toward him, wondering sarcastically how she'd gotten so lucky as to encounter one of her people on the vast expanse of beach.

It wasn't that Nacia disliked Frank. In fact, she liked him more than most of the men she came in contact with, and that encompassed a very large number. Not only was Frank one of the best salesmen her firm employed, he was, by nature, friendly and outgoing and had never given any indication that he resented the fact that his superior was a female. No, it was not dislike that caused Nacia's sigh, but merely her shattered hope of some solitude.

"Hi!" Frank grinned as she came up to him. "Are you on vacation, or just down for the weekend?"

"On vacation." Nacia's smile, though warm, lacked the brilliance of Frank's. She didn't have to ask the same question of him. Nacia knew Frank was not on vacation; he'd had his leave the last week of June and the first week of July. "Is Deborah with you?" she asked.

"Yeah." This time he smiled ruefully. "But not here on the beach. She can't take the sun. She freckles. Where's Tracy?" His head shifted as he glanced around quickly.

"In Florida," she answered without inflection. "With her father."

"Oh." Frank nodded; then a frown drew his bushy dark brows together. "You're down here on your own?"

Now Nacia sighed in exasperation. Frank was as bad as Tracy! What in the world did he think was going to happen to her, for heaven's sake? Was he afraid she'd be robbed, or raped, or something equally horrendous? Nacia smiled wryly through her annoyance.

"All on my own," she drawled dryly.

"But Nacia, it's not safe." Frank's frown deepened. "I mean, a woman like you, on your—"

"Can it, Frank, and introduce me to the lady."

The quiet, commanding voice that cut Frank off midspiel came from behind and below him. Slicing her glance to that totally male sound, Nacia let her eyes rest on a long, muscularly slender body reclining on a large navy blue beach towel. Her gaze, running up the length of him, came to a jarring stop when it reached his eyes; unbelievably, they were the exact same navy blue as the towel he lay upon, and they were coolly observing her.

Who was this man? Head jerking up and around, Nacia's eyes shot the question at Frank.

"Oh, yeah." Frank shook his head at his lack of courtesy. "Nacia, I'd like you to meet an old friend of mine, Jared Ranklin." As he spoke, the deeply tanned long body jackknifed upright and moved to stand beside him with a smooth agility that proclaimed more than a passing acquaintance with regular physical activity. "Jared, my boss, Nacia Barns."

Dark brows arched over those incredible navy blue eyes a fleeting instant before a long-fingered, broad hand was extended to her.

"Ms. Barns." There was a subtle difference in his tone, a hint of insinuation, a shade of sensuality. All he'd said was her name, yet Nacia heard the inflection and stiffened.

"Mr. Ranklin." The cool indifference of her tone was reflected in the brief, almost pressureless handshake she afforded him. He made no attempt to prolong the contact, yet Nacia experienced an odd sensation at the gentle pressure of his fingers against hers. She didn't like the feeling, and in an effort to dispel it she curled her fingers into her hand and drew her long nails over her palm.

She saw at once that her action had been a mistake, for his dark eyes followed the movement, and a tiny, knowing smile tugged at the corner of his mouth.

Suddenly Nacia was furious with him, with herself, with the hot sun that was causing a fine film of perspiration on her skin and a light-headed feeling that affected her balance. It had to be the heat from the sun; there was no other rational explanation for her dizziness. From start to finish, the entire incident had lasted mere seconds, yet Nacia felt exhausted, as if she'd gone without rest for days.

"Why don't you spread your towel over there, next to Jared's? It's one of the few remaining spaces on this section of the beach."

Nacia had been about to murmur the appropriate words of leave-taking when Frank issued his invitation. Glancing at him sharply, she thought wildly: Is the man mad? Couldn't he see? Of course he couldn't, for in reality there was nothing to see. Maybe she was the one who was going crazy!

Flicking a glance over the area, Nacia was faced with the truth of Frank's assertion; bodies in various degrees of relaxation littered the sand from waterline to boardwalk. It was either park next to the navy blue towel and its navy blue-eyed owner, or retreat to the motel. Retreat? Unthinkable!

Jared Ranklin had remained standing while Nacia made up her mind. When her gaze shifted from Frank's smiling face to Jared's patiently resigned expression, her hand dove into the capacious canvas bag. Before she had completely withdrawn her beach towel, he plucked it out of her hand.

"Allow me."

I wouldn't allow you the time of day! The retort trembled on Nacia's lips. Whatever was wrong with her? Nacia wondered in confusion as she mutely watched him shake out the length of terry and lay it beside his own. Chiding herself for her near violent reaction to the man, she drew the caftan up her body and over her head, unaware of the number of eyes, one pair navy blue, avidly observing the unconsciously sensuous movements.

By the time she had neatly folded the bright caftan, Jared was again in a prone position, as was Frank on the far side of him. Feeling slightly conspicuous, Nacia sank to the towel, her back to the men. Rummaging in her bag, she retrieved her bottle of sunscreen. Again with unintentional sensuality, she slathered the expensive coconut-scented oil on her legs, arms, shoulders, and upper chest, then paused, wondering how to coat her back; Tracy had always performed the small chore for her. Her mind was made up for her when the white plastic bottle was removed from her hand with a gentle tug.

"You forgot your back." Jared's dry tone left little doubt that he was well aware she'd forgotten nothing.

In rigid silence Nacia endured his touch. He began the application with long, firm strokes that imprinted the feel of his warm hand onto her skin. This was not the hand of an idle man or a pen pusher. No, the hand that drew shivers as it stroked her spine was rough textured and callused and filled with hard strength from physical labor. Gradually, the firm strokes changed to an enticing caress—a caress that awakened an evocative, long-dormant response in the essence of her femininity. She felt at once cold and hot, and suddenly very unsure of herself. When the hard tips of his fingers slid the hot oil down her side, then lingered to press provocatively into the full outer curve of her breast, she froze.

"That's enough!'

"Yes, it is," Jared agreed in a husky, amused drawl. "More than enough."

Nacia chose to ignore the double meaning in his soft assurance. She also attempted to ignore the tingling sensation in her breasts that was teasing her nipples into erection. As her attempt was an utter failure, she kept her back squarely to him.

Unnerved, Nacia tried to rationalize her reaction to him. It had been ages since a man had touched her anywhere, let alone that most sensitive of areas. A purely physical reaction, she reasoned. A biological response of all her female hormones to a blatantly attractive, obviously virile male.

Virile? Attractive? Nacia swallowed with difficulty. In the seconds he'd stood before her, his image had impressed itself on her memory. Yes, he was very, very attractive in a rugged, earthy way.

Unbidden, the image projected itself onto her inner eye. He was tall, somewhere in the area of six-one or two, and slender, especially from his narrow hips down; yet his chest, shoulders, and arms were flatly muscular. His head was well shaped and adorned with a thick crop of springy curls that had once been dark brown and now sported a natural frost. His forehead was broad and bore two shallow creases, as did his face from the outer edges of his long nose to the corners of his thin-lipped mouth. In all, he had a lean, angular look, not smooth or polished at all, and his eyes had that knowing expression that spoke of having experienced much and having been impressed by very little. His appeal, she decided dismissively, was to the senses, not the intellect.

"So, you're Frank's boss?"

Nacia felt a ripple of annoyance. She was sure she heard a too familiar insinuation in his tone. Another one who feels I worked my way into my job on my back, she concluded angrily. What an absolute bore men are; so damned predictable.

"Yes," she said coolly with a note of condescension in her voice. "I'm Frank's boss."

His soft, abrupt laughter deepened her annoyance; his observation fired her anger.

"Uh-oh, a militant feminist."

"Don't be absurd!" Twisting around, Nacia found herself glaring into eyes that held the devil's own taunt. He was stretched out on his flat middle, the upper part of his torso propped up on one elbow, his head cocked to look up at her.

"I try never to be absurd." His serious tone was belied by his dancing eyes. "You're not a militant feminist?"

Nacia felt trapped. She had never attended a meeting or carried a sign, but in truth, her feelings about men were pretty militant. Choosing her words carefully, she took a shot at his ego.

"I am a woman trying to make my way in a world that men like you have, by and large, screwed up."

He laughed!

Chapter 2

Nacia was sorely tempted to hit him! The intensity of the temptation shook her secure little world. Not even while she was living with and enduring Clay's abuse had she felt the urge to retaliate in a physical manner. Generally, outside of her necessary business relationships, she quite happily ignored most men. Aside from a few exceptions, Nacia considered men to be made up of fifty percent ego and fifty percent brawn. This particular man was definitely not one of the exceptions.

"Anyone for the water?" Frank's query cut through the tension shimmering between his beach companions. Innocently unaware of their antagonism, he shifted his gaze from the waterline to first Nacia, then Jared, his brows raised questioningly.

"Not me."

"Perhaps later."

Nacia smothered a groan as her voice blended in with Jared's; she had been certain he'd opt for the surf—if only to parade his slender maleness before all the avid man-hungry females cluttering the sand.

Frowning in consternation, she presented her back to Jared and watched Frank weave through the crowd on his way to the sea.

"God, I thought he'd never leave." Jared's mocking tone set her teeth on edge. "Now, where were we?" The sardonically voiced question was followed by the hard tip of his index finger sliding down her slippery spine. That touch set her entire body on edge. Jerking away from it, she slanted her most disdainful expression at him.

"*We* were nowhere!" she exclaimed furiously. "And don't touch me!"

"Why not?" His eyebrows, lifted theatrically. "When I was smearing that oil on your back, I discovered I enjoyed touching you." The skin at the corners of his eyes crinkled with amusement. "Even though I must admit there are other, more interesting sections of your anatomy I'd rather explore with my hands."

There was absolutely no way Nacia could repress the gasp that burst from her lips. This clown was really stuck on himself! Surely it was time someone brought him down a peg.

"You should live so long." Nacia smiled nastily as she spoke the scathing retort.

"Oh, it won't take long." The self-assurance in his tone was maddening. More maddening still was the languid way he lifted his hand to place his callused, roughened palm on the exposed skin in the valley between her breasts. "You're going to love it."

Sudden heat suffused her body. Stunned into immobility for a second, Nacia was fully aware that he felt the erratic kick as her heartbeat accelerated. Angry with herself as well as him, she leaned back precariously in a desperate effort to get away from the warm pressure of his hand. Was this man some kind of a sex maniac or merely crazy?

The conjecture sent her rocking to her feet. Frank's friend or not, she had to get away from this man!

"Running won't solve the problem."

His soft taunt halted her in midstride. Swinging around to face him, her eyes blazing with contempt, Nacia drew herself up to her full height, unconscious of the exciting appeal she exuded in her fury. In agitation she shook the mass of auburn waves off her face with a sharp movement of her head.

"I don't have a problem." Her eyes swept his lean frame. He was lying flat now, the upper part of his torso supported by his forearms. "If there is any problem, it is exclusively yours."

"I know," he surprised her by agreeing ruefully. "Why do you think I'm belly down on this damn beach?"

Seconds elapsed before his meaning became clear to Nacia, and the elapsed time was a clear indicator of exactly how very long it had been since she'd been subjected to any kind of sexual wordplay. With understanding came a mental image, followed by shock at her own erotic speculation.

Her sharply indrawn breath elicited a soft chuckle from below her.

"Don't let it throw you, beautiful. This too shall pass—for now."

That did it! Completely unnerved, Nacia grabbed her towel and her beach bag and fled, the sound of his delighted, self-satisfied laughter burning her ears all the way back to her motel.

Inside the safety of her room she flipped the lock in the knob and leaned back weakly against the smooth metal door. As her breathing returned to normal, she pushed sluggishly away from the solid support and walked on ridiculously shaky legs to the bed. Sinking onto the firm mattress, she stared blankly at her trembling hands.

Raising her head, she caught a glimpse of her own reflection in the dresser mirror opposite the bed. The dark brown gaze that stared back at her had a wary, haunted look that was in direct contrast to their usual cool, thoughtful expression. Unbidden, a vision of Jared Ranklin rose to her mind.

The trembling in her fingers increased as she lifted an oddly weak arm and placed her hand on the spot so recently covered by his. Her skin felt hot and vibrantly alive. A low moan tormented her throat as her eyes watched her breasts peak at the memory of his brief caress.

What was happening to her? Nacia grimaced at her image in scorn. Well, she knew *what* was happening, so the question was, *why* was it happening? Dammit, she'd consigned all those physical and emotional responses to the deep freeze ages ago. So why were they surfacing now? And in response to that bull of the woods, of all men!

"Oh, chit."

Nacia muttered Tracy's current term of disgust aloud, shaking her head in despair at the weak-fleshed woman gazing sadly back at her. Maybe she ought to go home, catch up on some reading as she'd told Tracy she was going to do. There were several sales manuals in her briefcase that she'd been planning to read while on vacation, or she could clean closets, or...

"Running won't solve the problem."

Jared's taunting voice echoed mockingly in her head. Double dammit, she would *not* allow that sexist gorilla the satisfaction of knowing he'd made her run!

But would he know it?

Nacia's shoulders straightened. Atlantic City was packed with vacationers, tourists and gamblers. With any luck at all she would not even set eyes on Mr. Jared Ranklin, chauvinist extraordinaire, during the remainder of her stay.

Soothed by that conclusion, she stood up and stretched luxuriously. Due to Tracy's departure, she had not slept well the night before; and she had wakened with the first fingers of sunlight that crept over the eastern horizon. What she needed was a nap.

Slipping out of her swimsuit, Nacia revised her thinking. What she needed was a warm shower and then a nap; the sunscreen oil had to go. Fat lot of good it had done her. She hadn't been in the sun long enough to get any color anyway!

Three hours later, refreshed from her deep, dream-free nap and dressed in a printed wrap skirt in shades of blue and green, a natural straw-colored gauze blouse, and high-heeled sling-back sandals, Nacia strolled to the boardwalk to catch the tram. Dinner

being the uppermost thought in her mind, and one of
the casino hotels her destination, she was oblivious to
the male glances that admired her loosely styled mass
of hair and the full, rounded maturity of her supple
body.

She ran the last few yards to the tram, which was
just leaving to make its return trip up the boardwalk.
Hopping into the open conveyance, Nacia paid the
fare and thanked the driver breathlessly for waiting for
her, again unaware of the gleam of admiration evident in his eyes as he assured her that it was his pleasure.

For the length of the trip Nacia's eyes observed the
undulating motion of the ocean, shimmering with
golden spangles from the long rays of the westering
sun. She was so enchanted with the sea's glittering,
hypnotic effect that the tram passed by the first two
hotels before she realized how far they'd come.
Alighting at the next stop, she waved at the grinning
driver and strode off toward the nearest hotel. She
encountered Frank and Deborah Evens at the boardwalk entrance.

Stepping aside so as not to impede foot traffic, the
three chattered through the usual greeting routine;
then, when Nacia mentioned she was in search of a
place to dine, both Frank and Deborah insisted she
join them. Apparently one of the hotel restaurants was
also their destination.

"We have reservations, but I'm sure they won't
mind one more." Frank's smile split his sunburned,
shiny face.

"Well . . ." Nacia hesitated, not wanting to intrude, but really not wanting to have dinner on her own either.

Slipping her arm through Nacia's, Deborah made the decision for her. "Come on, Nacia. We really haven't had a chance to talk for ages—not since the company Christmas dinner, actually." Slanting her a mischievous smile, she added, "We'll ignore the men and talk about our kids."

The men? Nacia opened her mouth to voice the question but was forestalled by Deborah as she launched into the topic nearest to her heart: her children.

Deborah barely paused long enough to draw breath when they arrived at the restaurant. "Oh, this *is* as lovely as our friends said it was," she said softly. "I hope the food is as good as they promised."

Smiling in understanding, Nacia's eyes casually swept the elegant decor of the large room. Her gaze settled on the maître d' as he came to a stop before Frank. Very impressive, she mused, studying the tall, rigidly erect blond man, who had the bearing of an aristocrat.

"One extra will be no inconvenience at all," the blond giant assured Frank smoothly. With a small, polite bow, he ushered them inside the dining room. "Follow me, please."

Suppressing a smile at the request, which sounded more like an order, Nacia turned her attention to Deborah, who was off and running again on her favorite subject. Other than to check where she was walking, Nacia did not look up again until they reached their table. When, laughing at the antics of the youngest Evens, she did turn her head, it was to find her glance caught—and held—by eyes so dark blue as to appear black.

Oh, chit! Luckily she did not mutter the words aloud, but why hadn't Frank mentioned the fact that Jared Ranklin was joining them for dinner? It was too late to chastise herself for not inquiring what Deborah had meant by "the men."

"Nacia?"

Jared's chiding, know-it-all tone ended her private lecture. Tearing her eyes from his, she came to the realization that he had moved behind the chair next to his own, his strong hands lightly holding the seat back in invitation.

For an instant Nacia considered making some sort of an apology and beating a hasty retreat. Pride refused to let her back up as much as a single step. The hell with him, she thought viciously. If I can't handle one big-headed man for the relatively short length of time required to consume a meal, I'll throw in the towel! Her confidence firmly in place, Nacia circled the table and accepted the proffered chair with a cool, "Thank you."

"Where did you disappear to this afternoon?" Frank's query came as Nacia settled into the comfortable chair. "When I came out of the water you were gone, and Jared here—" he tipped his head at his friend "—was sound asleep."

Before answering, Nacia slid a glance at Jared's bland expression. Sure he was; she silently labeled him a faker.

"I went back to my room for a nap." Nacia's shoulders lifted in a minishrug. "I just suddenly felt very sleepy. I didn't get much rest last night, and I was up very early this morning.'' The explanation was made with satisfying smoothness, revealing none of the tension beginning to gather along her nerves.

"Worried about the kid, were you?" Frank sympathized.

"Worried?" Deborah glanced in concern from her husband to Nacia. "Is something wrong with Tracy?"

"No, of course not." A strained smile stretched Nacia's beautifully formed lips. Merely thinking about Tracy spending two weeks with that man put a strain on her. She was totally unconscious of dark eyes watching and categorizing every nuance on her expressive face. "Tracy is spending two weeks in Florida with her father and his family." She smiled in self-derision. "She's never been away from home for that length of time before. It takes getting used to."

"Of course it does," Deborah concurred. "I remember when our firstborn went away to camp. I cried for three days!" Smiling mistily, she gazed at Jared. "I would imagine you know the wrench of parting more than any one of us, Jared!"

Nacia snapped to attention. What did Deborah mean? Why would he know more about parting from young ones than the two mothers at the table? Partial explanation came in an amused drawl.

"I've had my share. For sixteen years Joyce has bounced back and forth between her grandparents and home like a rubber ball." His thin, hard lips smiled ruefully. "It never seems to get any easier."

Although Nacia made a valiant effort to keep her face expressionless, her questions must have been evident, for Deborah hastened to enlighten her.

"Jared's been a widower for a long time now," she explained softly. "Ever since Linda died, his sixteen-year-old daughter, Joyce, has spent most holidays and every summer with Linda's parents."

"Oh, I see." Nacia scrupulously kept her tone free of inflection, all the while sure that what she saw was a man eager to unload his offspring at every opportunity.

"I doubt it."

So soft was the chiding retort, Nacia wasn't sure she'd heard him correctly. She was about to challenge him when their waiter stopped at the table and asked if they were ready to order. By the time the waiter departed, Frank had engaged Jared in a conversation on deep-sea fishing and the opportunity was gone.

Throughout the entire interminable meal, Jared subtly played on Nacia's nerves. Settling himself more comfortably in his chair, his thigh deliberately brushed against hers. While replacing his wine glass on the table, his subdued plaid sport coat just grazed the outer curve of her breast. While reaching to make a selection from the dessert cart, his lips barely brushed her ear.

"I want you."

Nacia became rock still. She *really* hadn't heard what she thought she'd heard, had she? Not even a bull of the woods would be so blatant, would he? Oh, wouldn't he? After his behavior on the beach that afternoon, Nacia felt sure this particular bull would say anything, the more outrageous the better.

Moving carefully, she shifted to the far side of her chair, her body pressed against the curved armrest. Impatiently, she endured the coffee and liqueur ritual, concentrating all her attention on Deborah. Would they never finish and call for the check?

Finally the move was made. Ignoring her demand to be told her share, Jared glanced at the total, then withdrew his wallet and placed several bills on the tray on which the check had been presented.

Nearly choking on her own words, Nacia thanked Jared for her dinner, her eyes skipping over the glittering sheen of amusement in the dark depths of his gaze. Holding on to her temper, she preceded him from the restaurant, intent on getting lost in the crush of people in the casino.

Appearing coolly contained on the outside, but a boiling mass of emotions on the inside, Nacia turned to bid farewell to her companions as they left the dining room; she wouldn't give the Evenses a chance to detain her.

"I'm for the tables," she announced with flat determination. "Dinner was lovely," she lied with aplomb. "If I don't run into you again before you leave, have a safe trip home. Frank, I'll see you in the office in two weeks." Turning, she leveled a haughty gaze on Jared. Politeness, good manners, nothing could induce her to say that meeting him had been a pleasure. Deliberately allowing her antipathy full play in her expression, she extended her hand. "Mr. Ranklin," she murmured when he gripped her hand with his own. "It's been...different." Hating the odd sensation caused by his warm, work-roughened palm grasping hers, she disengaged her hand quickly.

"It certainly has." Jared's dry tone mocked her cold front. "Good luck at the tables . . . Ms. Barns."

Nacia walked away swiftly. She had to. It was either get out of the vicinity fast or humiliate herself by taking a swing at him. The force of her emotional reaction to him astounded her. No one, male or female, had ever managed to rile her on such short acquaintance. It was unsettling and baffling, and Nacia was unfamiliar with both emotions. Striding into the casino she decided she could survive very easily without either of the feelings.

Hours later, having made healthy contributions to at least a dozen slot machines and one crap table, Nacia sat at a blackjack table contemplating her dwindling stock of chips. With a barely perceptible flicker of her fingers she indicated to the dealer that she was out of the play. Sliding off the low stool, she scooped up her few remaining chips and, jiggling them in her hand, began weaving her way through the crowd to the boardwalk exit; after hours of being confined in the crowded casino, fresh air was definitely called for.

Merely being outside was not enough. The muted sound of the sea drew her across the boardwalk to the rail, but somehow that was not enough either. The tide was out and the black expanse of moon-sprinkled water beckoned to her with its swishing siren song.

Unaccountably restless, Nacia succumbed to the impulse to follow that enticing tune. Choosing to ignore the fact that it was somewhere around two o'clock in the morning and probably unsafe for a woman alone, she descended the stairs to the beach, pausing on the bottom step to slip out of her sandals.

Her sling-back shoes dangling from her fingers, Nacia walked through the sand, leaving a direct line of footprints to the edge of the sea. The water lapping at her toes was cold, and with a tiny gasp she stepped back quickly. Laughing to herself as she hadn't done for years, Nacia turned and began walking south, every so often daring to step into the surf.

Caught up in a childlike world of her own, she was oblivious to the sounds from the boardwalk, the garish lights, everything.

"How the hell did you ever get to be the boss?"

With a small shriek, Nacia actually jumped, her sandals sailing into the air to land with a plop in the inky water.

"Good God, Jared!" Her voice had the high tightness of tension. "Are you crazy? You nearly scared me to death! What are you doing here?"

"More to the point, what are *you* doing here, and at two o'clock in the morning? Are you trying to get yourself rolled—or something worse?"

"Rolled?" Nacia eyed him with disdain. "How charming."

"I wasn't trying to be charming," he growled. Bending in a sweeping arc, he scooped her sandals out of the water. "I would have thought you were smart enough not to do a stupid thing like walking a deserted beach at this time of the morning." His harsh tone and his rigid stance revealed his tightly controlled anger. "How much have you had to drink tonight?"

Drink? This clod actually thought she was smashed! Counting to ten, Nacia slowly drew tangy salt air into her suddenly tight chest. This guy was really asking for it—and he was really going to get it!

"My alcohol intake is none of your business!" The blast came with the whooshing release of her breath.

"Nor is my walking the beach—at *whatever* hour. Get lost, Ranklin."

"I'm making it my business." Jared's soft voice held hard implacability. Ignoring her gasp of outrage, he grasped her arm and strode off toward the boardwalk, dragging her with him.

"Damn you. Let me go!" Nacia, panting, tried to yank her arm free without success. "Where are you going?"

"To find a cab," he answered calmly. "I'm taking you back to your motel. I don't want your ravishment on my conscience."

"My ravishment! You're insane. I swear, if you don't let me go, I'll... Oh!" Her breath caught as he came to a jarring halt at the foot of the steps leading up to the boardwalk.

"You'll what?" Jared challenged softly. "Scream? Slug me?" The light from the boardwalk bounced off his eyes, lending them the hard glittering look of sapphires. "Go ahead, but I must warn you. If you slug me, I'll probably retaliate in kind; and if you scream, I'll close your mouth with my own."

Through the haze of anger clouding her mind one thought registered clearly: Jared was not talking to hear the sound of his own voice; he meant every word he said. Even so Nacia could not ignore the need to defy him.

"Damn you," she gritted through clenched teeth, "you have no right to order me around."

"Right or not, I'm doing it." Jared's gleaming eyes mocked her impotent fury. "And you may damn me all you wish, I'm still seeing you safely back to your room." He paused to lift the hand holding her sandals. After giving the sodden leather a brief examination, he raised laughing eyes to hers. "I'm afraid you're going to squish a little when you walk, but—" he shrugged "—can't be helped. Sit down and I'll help you brush the sand off your feet."

Up until then Nacia hadn't even noticed the wet sand caked on her feet. Frowning, she glanced down, her gaze skimming her own feet before shifting to his. Wouldn't you know, she thought grumpily. He had ankle boots on. No sandy beach would impede *his* progress.

Dropping onto the third step from the bottom, she bent to the task, only to have her hand brushed away impatiently.

"Now what?" she snapped irritably. Glancing up, she discovered that his eyes were on a level with her own as he bent over her. Shaking out a neatly folded clean handkerchief, he swiftly and efficiently brushed the gritty sand off her skin. The touch of his work-roughened hands was surprisingly gentle and sent an odd heat rising from her instep to her thighs.

"Th-thank you." Shifting uncomfortably, Nacia drew her feet away from his disturbing ministrations. "That will suffice. If you'll hand me my sandals...please?"

"Shame." Though Jared's tone was rueful, his eyes mocked her obvious nervousness. "Just when I was beginning to enjoy the work, too." Disregarding her imperiously extended hand, he proceeded to slip the sandals onto her feet, grinning devilishly when she grimaced at the somewhat slimy feel of the wet leather.

Annoyed, frustrated, her mind seething with very unladylike but highly suitable words of censure, Nacia sprang to her feet.

"If you insist on this farce of gallantry, let's get it over with." Spinning away from him, she started up the steps, her teeth on edge at the sound of his low chuckle.

Before she had covered half the width of the boardwalk, Nacia had cause to regret her precipitous action. Traces of sand caught under the sodden leather grated against the sensitive skin on her feet. Laying the blame for her discomfort on Jared, she grimly strode on, determined not to betray herself by even the tiniest of winces.

When he procured a cab with very little effort, it only added to her irritation. Stepping with deceptive lightness into the back of the vehicle, Nacia slid to the very end of the seat and turned her face to the window.

"Where to, sir?"

Surreptitiously wiggling her toes in an attempt to ease the stinging chafe, Nacia heard, but did not register, the cab driver's question.

"Nacia, tell the man where we're going." Jared's amused voice abraded her nerves more than the sand had her skin. Without turning her head, she told the driver the name of the motel. Had she glanced around, she'd have caught the pleased smile that played over Jared's lips.

During the short run down Pacific Avenue, Nacia heard but did not absorb the sporadic remarks exchanged by Jared and the cabbie. She was tired and disgruntled and she also felt nervous and wary of the man sitting less than a foot away from her.

The fact that she was extremely bothered by Jared Ranklin puzzled her. Oh, Nacia was well aware of that nebulous emotion labeled physical attraction; even though she had not experienced it for over fourteen years, she was not unconscious of what went on around her. She had lost count of the times she'd shaken her head in despair at the friends who, having fallen victim to the urge to merge, sobbed out their subsequent unhappiness on her capable shoulders. The idea that those same friends might some day get the opportunity to shake their heads over *her* foolish behavior had never entered her mind.

The notion startled her into the realization of where she was and whom she was with. Feeling every muscle in her body growing tense with her wildly improbable conjecturing, Nacia made a concentrated effort to relax. There was not the slightest chance in the world of her falling victim to any man, most especially one whose attitude about women belonged in the Victorian era . . . was there?

The tacked-on question startled her. She had never even considered the possibility of being attracted to a man. Now, to find herself not only considering it but worrying over it to the point of stiffening all over was downright frightening. She must, she decided grimly, be even more tired than she'd originally thought. The day's events had done nothing to alleviate the months of accumulated tiredness. All she needed was rest—and to rid herself of the Cro-Magnon man she was with.

A sigh of sheer relief was on her lips as the cab glided to a stop in front of the quiet motel. Depressing the door handle, Nacia stepped out of the cab quickly, and immediately, wished she'd moved more carefully.

"Damn!" Nacia exclaimed, both at the pain in her feet and at the man who now stood beside her on the sidewalk. "Why didn't you keep the cab?" she demanded, glaring at the swiftly retreating vehicle.

"And leave you to hobble to your room without assistance?" Jared mocked while sliding one arm around her waist. "What kind of a gentleman would that make me?"

"I wasn't aware that you aspired to be *any* kind of a gentleman," Nacia retorted, unsuccessfully attempting to dislodge his arm.

"You wound me." Jared's grin belied his injured tone.

"For that I'd need an elephant gun," Nacia assured him nastily.

"Tsk, tsk. Sore feet making you sore all over?" he inquired with mock concern.

"Yes." Fully agitated, Nacia spat the confirmation at him. "It's your fault for sneaking up on me like an Indian."

"I was not consciously sneaking," Jared defended himself. "The tendency must be inbred."

Inbred? Now what was that supposed to mean? Concentrating on walking without flinching, Nacia dismissed the question as unimportant. She had a much more pressing matter to think about—that of getting to her room and removing her sandals.

Unable to shrug out of his possessive hold, Nacia resigned herself to being escorted across the dark courtyard to the concrete stairs that led to the second-level walkway. When, finally, they reached the door to her room, Jared released her. However, the relief she felt was short-lived. In an imperative tone, he demanded her key.

"I can manage, thank you—" she began.

"You can barely manage to stand up," Jared interrupted. "Stop arguing and give me the key, Nacia."

Nacia bristled at the note of command in his tone. What kind of vapid females has this clown been associating with? she wondered. Who cares? she answered her own silent query. Give him the damn key and get rid of him!

"You have visions of yourself astride a white charger?" Although she held the key out to him, she couldn't resist offering the barb with it.

"No." His suddenly glittering blue eyes pierced hers. "There are much more enjoyable objects to mount," he retaliated softly.

Nacia sucked in breath with a hissing sound. Objects? He thought of women as objects? Why should that surprise her? Distracted by her own thoughts, she was oblivious to his actions as he turned the key in the lock, then boldly entered the room.

"I thought you were in a hurry to get out of those wet sandals?" he taunted, holding the door wide open. "Do you require assistance?"

Biting back a sharp denial, Nacia stepped gingerly into the room. Hearing the door snap shut behind her, she spun around. The sudden movement caused friction between the wet leather straps and her sensitized skin. With a gasp of pain, she dropped onto the bed, eyeing Jared balefully.

"I don't recall inviting you in here," she snapped irritably, bending down to ease the offending sandals off her feet.

"Don't you?"

Nacia glared at him. Knowing the question to be rhetorical, she didn't bother answering the obvious.

"You would have preferred to have me kiss you out on the walkway?"

Now Nacia was incapable of answering. He was simply tormenting her—wasn't he? Her eyes probed his expression for reassuring evidence and found none. He was standing less than six feet away from her, and everything about him shrieked of self-confidence and determination.

"I *am* going to kiss you, you know." It was not a question. It was an assertion, issued so mildly that it sent a chill of apprehension up Nacia's spine. Sudden realization of her vulnerable position was the driving force that brought her to her now-bare feet.

"No, you are not." Every ounce of the disdain she felt for men weighted her deliberately spaced words.

"Actually, I think I've been very patient." His lips twitching with amusement, he walked to her slowly.

"What are you talking about? And stay where you are!" Not all the considerable willpower she possessed could keep the nervousness from her voice. Ignoring her order, Jared placed his long-fingered hands on her shoulders before answering her question.

"I'm talking about the patience I exerted over myself on the beach this afternoon while applying oil to your skin." As he spoke his eyes darkened with renewed desire. "I could almost taste you with my fingertips. I wanted to kiss you then, in front of anyone who cared to watch. It took an enormous amount of control not to." A rueful smile curved his lips. "I had to put that control to work again at the dinner table tonight."

His tauntingly whispered "I want you" of earlier that evening echoed alarmingly through her mind. Had she really convinced herself that he'd merely been trying to shock her?

Jared felt her shiver, and slid his hands soothingly over her shoulders and down her arms. "My control is getting pretty shaky, Nacia."

Anger ripped through Nacia as he lowered his head. Consumed with the need to get him out of her room, she launched an ill-considered verbal attack.

"You overbearing, pompous ass," she blazed scathingly. "Get out of here at once. Go try your Neanderthal act on some simpering pea brain. I'm unimpressed by it."

Retaining his hold on her arms, Jared went rigidly still, fine lines of strain etching his face as the color drained out of it.

"Overbearing? Pompous? Ne-an-der-thal?" Up until now, his tone had been teasingly amused. Now it contained a deadly note that closed Nacia's throat with sheer panic. "You want Neanderthal?" he rasped, his eyes nearly black with fury and passion. "I'll give you Neanderthal."

"Jared . . . no!"

Paralyzed by the swiftness of his move, Nacia stood, immobile with shock as his lips savaged hers. The invasion of his stiffened tongue shattered her brittle stillness. Twisting convulsively, she attempted to free herself from the hard fingers that gripped her upper arms, rendering them useless in her struggle. All her effort achieved was to bring her body into contact with his, inflaming him even more.

Hungrily, he pushed her back on to the bed, his mouth still clamped to hers. The force of his body striking hers set off an explosion of her senses, and for several seconds Nacia was beyond resistance as she felt her blouse, then her wraparound skirt being removed from her body by hard, impatient hands. As her mind began to catch up to her senses, she became aware of her instinctive response to the touch of Jared's lips against the side of her neck, the harshly ragged sound of his labored breathing. When her lacy bra followed her other clothes to the floor, and his hand slid from her arm to her breast, a spasm shuddered through her body—a spasm caused by both fear and pleasure.

"Jared—stop!" Nacia's voice held panic, instilled more by the unfamiliar sensation of physical pleasure than by fear.

"It's too late." A strange note of self-condemnation laced his raspy voice. "I must have you now, Nacia. You can't tell me that you want me to stop."

She couldn't, and yet she must try to stop him. His hand released her breast, and a moment later she heard the faint scrape of metal as he tugged open his belt buckle.

The weight of his broad bared chest—when had he shed his jacket and shirt?—prevented any defensive movement from her. When she heard the metallic sound of his descending zipper, she instinctively moved to insert her knee between his muscle-tautened thighs.

Jared didn't waste time or energy on cautionary words. Moving with a swiftness she would not have believed possible, he avoided her leg while at the same time divesting himself of slacks and cotton briefs.

"Jared, please . . . Oh!" Nacia's protest was caught up in a gasp as, simultaneously, his hand moved caressingly over her now-naked body and his mouth captured hers in a devastatingly gentle kiss.

Her hand pushed ineffectually against the curves of his rib cage as she tried to voice her confusion. Nacia went rigid as Jared lowered his lean frame between her thighs.

In that instant of stillness Nacia was keenly aware of the hardness of his body, the harshness of his breathing, the rough texture of his hands on her skin, and the male scent of him filling her nostrils.

He murmured something unintelligible directly into her mouth, and with renewed vigor Nacia pushed at his body, writhing in an effort to press herself into the mattress away from him.

When it happened, it was like a flash fire burning out of control, consuming everything in its path. The needs and emotions Nacia had ruthlessly suppressed for far too many years broke free and ran amok through her system, overriding objection, outrage and common sense.

Hungrily, greedily, she arched herself to his piercing masculinity. Jared responded forcefully, taking everything she had to give, giving everything of himself in return.

Chapter 3

"*M*en and their damned macho mentality."

Nacia flung the angry indictment at the ceiling. Though she meant every word of the condemnation, she was well aware that it was a cop-out.

Jared had come on to her like Attila the Hun. He had, at least figuratively, backed her into a corner. With his superior strength, he had left her two options: submit or suffer. He had had no way of knowing Nacia would create a third option—that of voluntary contribution. There was no way he could have known, for Nacia had not known it herself.

The entire scene had required mere moments to complete. Moments during which the only sounds in the room were his harshly labored breathing and her gasping moans of pleasure.

Now, with her own breathing slowing to normal, Nacia stared at the gray-white ceiling and faced the fact that she'd been an active participant in their lovemaking.

It was conscience-shattering.

It was degrading.

It was disgustingly satisfying.

The realization that she had enjoyed Jared's rough lovemaking had made her turn on him, and all of the old bitterness she felt against her ex-husband came flooding back.

"Macho mentality." Jared repeated the phrase consideringly. "What, exactly, is that supposed to mean?"

Not bothering to turn her head to look at him, Nacia answered. "Exactly what it says," she sneered. "The condescending, muscle-flexing attitude males have had since day one. Me Tarzan, you Jane. I am physically superior, therefore I must have been granted the divine right to bonk her over the head and drag her into the cave." She was unaware, and uncaring, of Jared's dark eyes intently studying her rigid profile and scornfully curled lip.

"Ho, boy," Jared breathed softly. "You *are* carrying an overload of hate."

"And you've just fanned the flames."

"I did not force you, Nacia." Jared's soft tone took on an impatient edge. "I know I came on a . . . a little strong at the beginning, but . . ."

"There's always a but, isn't there?" Not about to listen to him remind her of her own stupidity, Nacia sprang to her feet. Unmindful of her nakedness, she stared at him, her eyes filled with derision. "I'm going to take a shower. I fully expect you to be gone by the time I'm out." Her face free of expression, she turned away from him.

"Nacia."

Ignoring the shiver caused by the entreating sound of his voice, Nacia walked unfalteringly into the bathroom, closing the door quietly before springing the lock with a final-sounding click.

Carefully avoiding her reflection in the mirror above the fitted vanity sink, she removed her makeup with cleansing cream before washing her face, then scrubbing her teeth in an effort to remove the bitter taste in her mouth. Then, after turning on the faucets in the molded fiberglass shower bath, she stepped into the spray, praying that by the time she was through her room would be empty.

Blanking her mind to everything but her plea for his departure, Nacia stood under the jet spray of hot water until the rising steam made her light-headed and the wet heat reduced her muscles to the consistency of rubber. Another five or so minutes were consumed by slowly patting herself dry. When she could procrastinate no longer, she slipped into the short, lightweight wrap she'd hung on a hook on the inside of the door that morning.

Looping the tie belt snugly, Nacia straightened her shoulders, drew a deep calming breath, and opening the door, walked aggressively into the bedroom. After gearing herself up for a confrontation, it was anticlimactic to discover that Jared had followed her order to remove himself.

One minute she was standing erect, tall, and proud, her eyes snapping with challenge; then weariness struck, deflating her spirit, dulling her eyes and robbing her of all defenses.

Nacia's sweeping glance came to rest on the bed, eyes narrowing as they encountered the rumpled spread. On entering the room yesterday, she had thought the covering beautiful. Now, the rich gold color that had reminded her of a particularly spectacular sunset was an affront to her senses.

Lips twisting with distaste, Nacia strode to the bed. Grabbing a handful of the textured material, she yanked the cover from the bed, dropping it carelessly onto one of the room's two occasional chairs.

That small flurry of activity exhausted her. Listlessly removing her robe, and too tired to bother putting on a nightgown, Nacia slid naked between the cool percale sheets, biting her lips against the need to cry even as the hot moisture welled up to sting her eyes.

The last of her barriers dissolving in a flood of tears, she turned her face into the pillow and sobbed. After all this time, how had it happened? Why had it happened? Nacia sniffed ineffectually, then sniffed again before pushing the covers back and sitting up to glance around distractedly for her handbag.

Not surprisingly, she found her purse exactly where she'd dropped it, on the floor beside the bed. Brushing impatiently at her wet cheeks, she scooped the bag off the carpet and withdrew a small packet of tissues. It was at that moment that Nacia realized she'd crawled into bed with the lights on.

Sighing wearily, she slid off the mattress and padded across the room to switch off the lights that Jared had turned on earlier. Even though Nacia knew it was impossible, she imagined she could feel the warmth of his fingers on the cool, impersonal plastic; with trembling fingers, she flipped the switch quickly, as if in fear of an electrical shock.

For some strange reason, turning the light off seemed to turn the waterworks on again. With the resumption of the tears and the sniffles, she dashed back to the bed to burrow under the covers.

The sudden movement brought the realization that she was sore in at least a dozen places on her body.

"Savage bastard!"

Gingerly Nacia explored each of the tender areas. Her mouth felt seared and swollen; the sensitive skin on the side of her neck was abraded from the friction of Jared's stubble; her ribs ached, as did her thighs.

Jared had in no way spared her. God, who would have ever conceived of the power contained within that slender form? Tingling, her palms again knew the feel of the rippling, corded muscles of his shoulders, his back, and most shamefully, his hips and buttocks.

Growing warm from her toes to the roots of the hair on her head, Nacia squirmed restlessly, her body awakening with the memory of his life force.

How she hated him! And yet how she ached anew with the need to enclose his supple strength within her arms and her legs, and the very essence of her being!

What in hell had happened to her? The question was a thorn that pricked her conscience. Hadn't she slammed the door over a decade ago on all things even remotely tinged with sensuality? Hadn't she repressed every one of her physical urges during that time? And the damnable thing was, she had won! She could not

even remember the last time the stirrings of her trai-
torous body had made her vaguely uncomfortable.

Now, within hours of meeting this...this cretin, she
had succumbed after the merest token of resistance. It
was unendurable.

Writhing with the conflicting emotions of intense
physical arousal and scorching psychological shame,
Nacia became entangled in the bedcovers. Uncomfortably hot and sticky, she agitatedly pushed back the
covering.

At first, the cool air from the window unit felt like
a balm as it flowed over her flushed skin.. Then, an-
noyingly, the effect was reversed. As her skin cooled,
the air whispered over her body like caressing fingers.

Work-roughened fingers? Nacia groaned in protest
at the instantaneous tautening of her breasts, the anticipatory quivering of their tight, crowning buds, the
melting heat of her body's core.

Why? The anguished cry boomed without surcease
through her mind while her inflamed senses tormented her body.

Without exception, she had coolly withstood the
blandishments of men more handsome, more polished, more attuned to her own personality.

Jared Ranklin was everything she despised. He was
too smugly confident of his superiority, too patroniz-
ing, to blatantly masculine.

Why, then, had it been *this* man? Wasn't he the
personification of everything she disdained in the human male? Yes, he was. Curled now into a tight ball
of misery, Nacia condemned Jared bitterly before
turning that bitterness on herself.

So why had she yielded?

There was no answer. Indeed, though she taxed herself repeatedly during the long hours that followed, no answers presented themselves. She could find no logical reason to explain and excuse her self-betrayal.

Through the dark hours Nacia swung back and forth between the sweats and the chills, alternately pushing the covers away and pulling them up to her chin. It was a long, long, sleepless night.

In his motel room Jared was having a running battle with himself.

Sprawled naked on the bed, his arms flung wide, he relived the previous hour, not only in his mind, but in every cell, nerve, bone and muscle in his body. His mind strove to reject the memory; his body exulted in it.

But you practically attacked her, he accused himself. *No!* I did not! Jared argued with the voice of his conscience. I threw her down, yes, but I never would have forced her.... I didn't *have* to. He frowned in the darkness. What had happened to her, there at the last moment? A vision filled his mind, then his body, and Jared shivered from the intensified ache in his loins. God! How he longed to bury himself inside the sweetness of her again.

But you hurt her! His head moved restlessly on the pillow. Yes, I hurt her. And now I'm hurting. Big deal! his conscience sneered. Rape is never permissible. Rape is an abomination. You raped her, if only in intent. *Her!*

Chilled, Jared shuddered and flung one sinewy arm over his eyes, as if hoping to block out the scenes that were swirling inside his head.

Nacia.

The silent cry filled his consciousness, obliterating all other sounds, inside or out. *Nacia. I can't even ask for forgiveness, because I cannot feel sorry for having had you.*

Thinking about the act brought visions of it. Groaning softly, sweating with the effort to keep his body from writhing in need, Jared quietly made a vow.

"I will have you again. I won't hurt you, my darling, I swear it, but I will have you."

God! What an arrogant beast you are! Jared's conscience was back, like a razor-tongued shrew. *You try that macho-man performance again and she'll probably run out, buy a gun, and blow you right to hell.*

Jared's drawn features moved in a parody of a smile. *To have her again, it just might be worth it.*

He lay there feeling tired yet restless for several seconds, then decided to expend some of the pent-up frustration he was feeling. *Enough with the fruitless mental and physical squirming,* he decided. *Move out, lover boy.*

Fifteen minutes later, in a whirling mist that was not yet a real, honest-to-goodness rain, Jared went running silently down the beach in quest of peace from his nagging conscience.

He hadn't noticed that the void deep inside him was now filled.

Near dawn, unable to bear the confinement or the bed another minute, Nacia fought her way out of the tangle of sheets and blankets.

Hurriedly she slipped into brief panties and bra, well-worn jeans and a baggy T-shirt, then slid her feet into rubber flip-flops.

As she transferred the contents of the small purse she'd carried the night before to her more practical, roomy shoulder bag, Nacia shot a rueful glance at her reflection.

God, she was a mess! Her hair was every bit as tangled as the bedclothes. Her face was totally devoid of color. Lines of strain etched the corners of her eyes and mouth, and blue shadows smudged the tender skin beneath her eyes. Her shoulders sloped as if under an enormous weight. Grimacing at the unappealing picture she made, Nacia reached for her hairbrush.

"Is this the face that launched a thousand ships?"

The bitter, self-mocking sound of her voice bounced off the silvered glass as Nacia attacked her hair with the brush.

"More like the mug that sank a thousand tugs."

Having thus dismissed the way she looked, she twisted the now-smooth mass of hair into a loose knot on the top of her head, securing it with a long silver barrette.

Turning away from the mirror, she hooked the bag's leather strap over her shoulder and walked to the door, only to stop abruptly upon swinging it open.

It was not yet fully light. It was chilly. It was raining. Great, Nacia decided bleakly. It was the ideal weather to match her mood.

A few minutes later, wearing a hip-length poplin jacket, a paper-thin plastic rain bonnet covering her head, Nacia closed the door to her room behind her and went along the wet walkway to the stairs.

Making her way to the street, Nacia turned in the direction of the boardwalk, grateful for the absence of traffic—both vehicular and pedestrian. Thanks to the earliness of the hour and the dreariness of the weather, she didn't pass a soul all the way to the boardwalk.

Even the famous promenade, eerily blanketed in a grayish mist rolling inland off the sea, was lacking in life except for the gulls, and one lone figure sitting on the topmost rail on the ocean side of the walk.

Nacia was halfway across the boards before recognition dawned and she froze in place. The lone man was the last person she wanted to meet with this morning.

Jared Ranklin!

Of course. Who else would she encounter on a chilly, rainy morning? The rest of the populace were still hiding under their comforting covers, warm and dry—all, that is, except Jared Ranklin, damn his hide.

From where she stood she viewed him in profile, and something about his posture stirred a fleeting memory. For the life of her, Nacia could not identify exactly who or what he reminded her of.

His back ramrod straight, Jared sat facing the horizon. Even from a distance, Nacia could see that his face was set in hard, uncompromising lines. His jawline had a taut, bunched-up look, as if from tightly clenched teeth.

His jogging jacket, cutoff jeans, and scuffed sneakers failed to camouflage the essence of the man. To Nacia's admittedly prejudiced eyes he projected an implacable male strength, fierce pride, and a savage arrogance.

Nacia's narrowed lids widened. That was it! The arrogance of a savage! At that moment his harshly outlined, dark-skinned, supremely proud appearance reminded her of every impression she'd ever harbored of a fierce-looking American Indian.

Either your mind is very tired or you're losing it, she scoffed to herself. Or, worse still, you're beginning to hallucinate! Savage indeed! He's a man. One, moreover, who is prey to his own unbridled passions.

Her gaze skimmed over him again, noting his superior, Lord-of-all-I-survey pose. Snorting softly, Nacia spun around. In her opinion he was barely worth the room he took up on that precarious rail perch.

She had retraced several of her own steps when she brought herself up short. Was she going to scurry back to her room and hide? She had escaped that cell-like accommodation to walk and think by the calming sound of the sea. She would not be sent into retreat by a mere man—especially *that* man.

Nacia prudently walked south along the inland edge of the boardwalk for a couple of blocks before crossing the boards to the steps that descended to the beach, hoping to lose herself from view in the now thick white fog.

She might as well have spared herself the effort of stealth. Her bare feet had barely made contact with the sand when the softly called sound of her name arrested her motion.

"Nacia."

Nacia imagined she could actually feel her blood drain from her head, and she became perfectly still in fear of toppling over. Maybe, just maybe, if she didn't move or respond in any way, he might take the hint and go away.

And the sand beneath her feet might turn into grains of pure gold, too. Nacia smothered a bubble of frantic laughter.

"Nacia?"

Nacia's muscles contracted stiffly, her sharply indrawn breath became trapped midway between the back of her throat and her chest. She had not heard the slightest rustling, yet the evidence of his movement assailed her ears in the form of his lowered tone, and her nostrils in the distinctly male scent of him. In an effort to still the quivers washing over her in ever-increasing waves, she curled her hands into tight fists, oval nails punishing her tender palms.

"Go away, Ranklin." The very rawness of Nacia's voice betrayed her tension. The use of his last name conveyed her contempt.

"We have to talk."

He was standing so close she could feel his warm breath on the skin on the back of her neck. Suddenly, the simple exercise of breathing in and out became an ordeal. Her flesh cringing, Nacia shook her head sharply in denial—not only of his calm assertion but of his presence as well.

"Yes, we do," Jared insisted gently, "and you know it."

"No!" Although she had hoped never to have to see his face again, Nacia was goaded into swiveling around to him. Oh, God, she despaired, why did he have to look so damned good? And how had he managed to instill that deceitfully tender glow in his eyes? "No," she repeated harshly. "We have nothing to talk about. You said it all . . . physically last night."

"Okay, I'm a Neanderthal with a macho mentality," he sighed. "But—and yes, in this case there *is* a but—I swear I did not mean that to happen...at least not that way." Impatience warred with the tenderness in his gaze. "Nacia, I..." Lifting his hand, he touched her arm lightly. Her reaction was immediate and violent.

"Don't touch me!" Nacia's snarl had a feral sound; her movement as she jerked away from him was reminiscent of a cornered animal. How often had she sneered at the use of the oh-so-trite phrase when reading it in a novel or hearing it while watching a TV show or a play? She was not given time to wonder, for Jared's reaction was every bit as swift as her own.

"For God's sake, Nacia, I'm not going to hurt you!" he said impatiently.

"You already have!" Nacia retaliated shrilly.

"I know," Jared conceded tiredly. "I know." The hand that she'd shrugged away found the back of his neck, long fingers digging into corded muscles. "Look, I'm not going to quit." His lips curved into the merest shadow of an apologetic smile. "I can't. Not now." The breadth of his flatly muscled chest expanded, then contracted slowly. "Let me walk with you." He held up his hand as Nacia's head began a side-to-side motion. "Walk and talk with you, Nacia, that's all. I promise I won't make any overt moves or touch you."

"And I'm supposed to be impressed by your promise?" Nacia's attempt at ridicule didn't quite make it, possibly because the way his face tightened cut off her laughter. Narrowed eyes and the way he rubbed his palms over the denim clinging to his hips were unmistakable warning signs that she was on very precarious ground in challenging his given word. Holding her breath, she took one cautious backward step, aware that if this man struck her she'd go down for the count.

"Dammit! Don't flinch from me like that!" The anger was back, full-blown and terrifying; it dissipated as swiftly as before. "Nacia, will you please turn around and start walking—in whatever direction you wish?"

"How about Europe?" Somehow she had contrived a cool tone that was reinforced by an expressively arched brow.

Oddly, confusingly, her taunt brought him to a full stop. His stillness was nearly as frightening as his anger. Then slowly, Jared shook his head.

"You caught me on that barb," he admitted ruefully. "For a moment there, I actually considered the possibility that you had come to the beach at this ungodly hour with self-destruction in mind." His piercing stare held Nacia's unwilling gaze. "No," he almost crooned, "not you. You are much too arrogant to ever contemplate self-destruction." Her soft gasp earned a slashing white grin. "You may have considered knocking me off," he allowed teasingly, "but never yourself."

Frustration grating at her lack of a retort, due perhaps to his astute assessment of her character, Nacia pivoted and set off walking across the sand. Within seconds he was right behind her, then beside her, carefully keeping a gap of eight to ten inches between them.

Sublimely unconcerned that the rain was beginning to soak through her jacket, or that the first and second fingers of her left hand were growing numb from gripping the thongs on her flip-flops, Nacia trudged on doggedly through the wet sand, trying with little success to ignore the silent man pacing her.

After walking south for several blocks, she turned to the sea, cautiously testing the water temperature with the toe of one foot. His feet still sneakered, Jared hung back a few inches from the foam left by the receding wavelets.

"Did you get any sleep at all?"

Even though Nacia had been waiting tensely for him to speak, the quiet sound of his voice startled her, and spinning around, she splashed water onto her jeans, soaking the legs from midcalf down.

"No," she admitted honestly, stepping daintily from the surf.

"It shows," he said bluntly.

Although Nacia assured herself she couldn't be less interested in his opinion of her appearance, her tone burned with sarcasm. "How very gallant."

"You want gallant, or the truth?"

Nacia had always thought of her eyes as a very ordinary brown, never realizing that when she was genuinely amused or fighting mad, the amber flecks that sprinkled the brown glittered like pure gold. For some inexplicable reason, Jared's taunt made her very mad, and the amber flecks shot sparks at him.

"I want nothing from you." Proud of her strong tone, Nacia drew herself up to her full height and stared directly into his eyes. The way his navy blue gaze darkened should have warned her of retaliation and the form it would take.

"Strange," he said sardonically. "For a few minutes there last night—or earlier this morning—you wanted something very badly from me." His gaze bored into her relentlessly.

Nacia's gasp was so loud it startled a nearby bird into flight. "You . . . you . . ."

"SOB?" Jared murmured helpfully. "Perhaps. But I've been around a long time—forty-one years, actually—and I know the difference between passive acceptance and active participation." His eyes flared with remembrance. "You were one very hungry lady."

The accuracy of his charge shamed Nacia and set her cheeks on fire. Never had she met such a tactless beast! Grimly determined not to reveal how deeply his barb had penetrated, she lifted her chin.

"And you've convinced yourself that my . . . ultimate response absolves your earlier behavior?"

"No." Jared grimaced in obvious self-disgust. "No, Nacia, I'm fully aware that not only is there no absolution, there is no defense for my lack of control."

As she'd been mentally gearing herself to demolish any argument he presented in his own defense, Nacia felt suddenly deflated, and very tired.

"Then why did you insist we had to talk?" she sighed. "What you did cannot be undone." Without conscious thought she moved her free hand dismissingly. "There is nothing to talk about."

A bright spark of anger glowed fleetingly in his eyes and he took one step toward her before coming to an abrupt halt.

"Yes there is!" he exclaimed harshly. "I want to try and explain—not defend, but explain what motivated my actions." His eyelids narrowed. "And I'd like to hear your explanation for yours."

He had neatly trapped her. She knew it. Jared knew it, too.

"Fourteen years of suppression." Obeying an overriding impulse to justify her conduct, Nacia tossed the statement at him rashly. She was immediately sorry for her reckless honesty.

"You're putting me on!" His skeptical expression, the patent disbelief in his tone, sent a shiver through her that had nothing to do with the chill from her rain-soaked jacket. "I was there, remember? I felt the passion driving you. You expect me to believe that I'm the first man you've been with in over a decade?"

Nacia was tired and beyond verbal fencing; it showed in her voice. "I don't care what you believe. I don't care what you think. I don't care what you feel." Her sigh spoke volumes about her weariness. For the moment her anger was spent; she was simply too tired to maintain it. "No matter how you slice it, you forced your way into my room and took me. I had nothing to say about it."

The final thrust hurt. It was there for her to witness in the spasm of pain that worked its way across his face, clouding his eyes, compressing his lips into a straight line. Oddly, it was then she noticed how perfectly those lips were shaped.

"You go straight for the jugular, don't you?" The rawness of his voice mirrored his expression; he was hurting, and she was glad. Lifting her head proudly, she met his reproachful stare straight on.

"It's your turn to suffer."

"My turn!" His snort of laughter had a hollow, dead ring. "What the hell do you think I did all night? Laugh myself silly? Pat myself on the back?" He closed his eyes briefly, and when he opened them again they were opaque with torment. "Nacia, I have never before used force on a woman. I...I..." He shook his head as if to dispel confusion. The movement sent droplets flying from the now-sodden ringlets that covered his head.

"God, it's pouring!" Jared's lips twisted with the wonder of it. His gaze sharpened on her shivering form. "You're wet through, and you're cold. Let's get off this beach and find some hot coffee."

Nacia stiffened as he reached out to lightly clasp her upper arm. Two separate longings rose in conflict. One was to shrug off his hold and tell him to go to hell. The other was to wrap her chilled fingers around a steaming mug of coffee. The need for a bracing dose of caffeine won hands down. Still, she felt the need to make her feelings known.

"All right, I'll have coffee with you. I'll even listen to your explanation. On one condition."

"Name it."

"You will then walk away and leave me alone."

Jared's hesitation was barely noticeable.

"Okay. If you still want me to."

Adjusting his long stride to hers, being careful to keep a few inches of space between them so that even their jackets did not brush, Jared studied the proudly lifted head and clean profile of the woman beside him.

Though well-defined, the features proportionately correct, there was nothing extraordinary about her face. All the same, it was the only face he cared to gaze upon. Jared had not felt quite this way about a woman in a very long time, if ever.

Nacia didn't deign to show she noticed his obvious perusal, her only indication of awareness of his examination a slight tightening of her color-free lips.

A tiny near-smile twitched at Jared's mouth. Damn, even all drawn in and closed looking, her lips set up a chain reaction inside his body, creating the urge to do all kinds of things to her—with her. A very definite effort was required to contain the twitch at the corners of his mouth.

Cool it, boy, he advised himself, only half seriously. Take it slow, take it easy, and hopefully you can take it all. She's hungry, you know that; but now you must make her hungry for you personally.

A shiver of anticipation went skittering down Jared's spine. God! He had to do it; he had to make her aware of him as a person, as a man, as the *only* man for her.

At the moment, she was vacuum-packed, like a can of coffee, sealed tight against feeling any kind of emotional response. Applied force would not release the pressure, he knew that.

So, Jared fought to control a grin; he would be the world's best can opener!

Chapter 4

The brightly lighted coffee shop was an empty haven at six forty-five on a storm-tossed morning.

"Morning, folks. Coffee?" The plump middle-aged waitress smiled at them.

"Yes, please." Jared answered for both of them as Nacia was occupied with removing her plastic rain hat and soaking jacket.

Not until the jacket was hung on the coat hook at the end of the booth did she realize her error. Her damp T-shirt clung to her body, clearly revealing the lacy nothingness of her bra. Turning from the waitress, Jared's gaze caught, became riveted on the chill-hardened tips of her breasts pointing directly at him.

The sudden alert intensity of that dark blue gaze created an unwelcome yet unmistakable fission of arousal deep inside Nacia. She hated it, but was unable to control the quiver that feathered her skin, tautening the proud mounds.

"God, I want to touch you!" Jared's involuntary exclamation came on a strangled whisper.

Nacia wanted to protest, deride, chastise. She wanted to, but could not. Ensnared in the blue depths of the eyes that had lifted to hers, she trembled with a sudden passion that was primitive in nature, making her ache for the feel of his callused hands.

The arrival of the waitress bearing steaming cups of coffee and two plastic-encased menus broke the strange, unsettling spell.

"I'll be back in a minute for your orders," she chirped, swinging away to attend to a lone male customer who had moments before entered the shop.

"Confusing, isn't it?"

Nacia was startled out of her introspection by Jared's mildly voiced observation. What in the blazing hell was happening to her? There was no answer to her silent cry. None that she was prepared to face, at any rate. His soft question echoed loudly inside her head. Nacia scurried down the path of denial through ignorance.

"I don't know what you're talking about."

An unnervingly gentle smile softened the hard male lips.

"Yes, you do," he chided, "but we'll leave it for now." His gaze shifted to the menu in his hands. "How do you want your eggs?"

"In the carton. In the refrigerator."

An appreciative smile saluted her caustic humor.

"Cereal? Pancakes? Waffles?"

"Yuck."

Fighting the lure of his smile, Nacia gripped the cup with both hands and raised it to her lips. The hot brew scorched her tongue. Blinking away the tears that rushed to her eyes, she focused on the glass of ice water Jared held aloft.

"Thank you."

"You're welcome." He studied her as she soothed the sting with the cold liquid. "Better?" At her nod, he wiggled the menu. "You should eat something, if only some toast."

"All right," she sighed. "I'll have a toasted English muffin."

"And some juice," he prodded softly.

Nacia gritted her teeth. What was she doing here? she wondered angrily. And with this man? She sneezed. Perhaps she'd better have a shot of vitamin C.

"And some juice—grapefruit."

Had he dared to smile, she'd have flung her coffee cup at him.

Jared didn't smile, at least not at Nacia. He did smile at the waitress as he relayed their order. The waitress loved it. For good reason, too, Nacia admitted grudgingly. His smile was rather devastating. Turning back to face her, the smile disappeared.

"Explanation time?" Lowered, his voice had a gravelly sound.

"If you must." Nacia contrived a note of boredom. In actual fact she was beginning to feel panicky. She didn't want to talk about it. She didn't even want to *think* about it. Most especially her part in it.

"As I said before, I had not planned on—" a tiny pause "—what happened."

"And that exonerates you?" Nacia gave in to the urge to strike at him verbally.

"No, dammit! I—" Jared bit off whatever he was about to say as their cheerful waitress approached with their order.

"I told you I would not defend myself," he continued when they were once again alone. "I am fully aware that there is no defense for what I did." He jabbed his fork into the creamy scrambled eggs on his plate. "I don't know what the hell happened." Lifting the fork, he transferred its cargo into his mouth. A frown creasing his brow, he chewed methodically. "I had planned to kiss you—several times. And I had planned on sharing a bed with you—eventually." The fork-to-mouth process was repeated automatically, unconsciously. The crease in his brow deepened.

"Nacia, I told you I've never forced myself on a woman." For the first time since he'd begun eating Jared raised his eyes to hers. "You have to believe me. I don't know why I lost all control with you!"

His whispered cry held pure anguish. Nacia swallowed the bit of muffin she'd been chewing to death, and felt it scrape all the way down her suddenly dry throat. Grabbing for her cup, she gulped the last of her coffee.

His breakfast forgotten, he stared directly into her eyes. "I wanted you. I admit that. I still do. But there is no defense, no rationale that will excuse the use of force." His lips twisted in self-derision. "If another man tried it with you, I'd want to kill him."

Nacia pressed back against the booth, her eyes widening in fear. "Are you crazy?" It was not until the words were spoken that she questioned their wisdom.

Now he did smile at her. "No, Nacia." He shook his head. "I'm not crazy. At least I wasn't the day before yesterday."

"Meaning?"

"I saw something I wanted. I went after it. Too hard. Too fast. Result?" His smile grew sad. "Instant stupidity."

"And now you want me to forgive you?" she ventured softly.

"No!" Jared's denial came swiftly, harshly. "Because I'm still not sorry it happened."

Nacia's mouth dropped open in amazement. Here she'd been on the verge of feeling something akin to compassion for him, and he tosses one at her from left field!

Get out of here, Nacia, she advised herself; this guy is strictly off-the-wall. His voice stopped her cold as she began inching across the bench seat.

"Now I'd like to hear your explanation."

Nacia had always considered the phrase "my blood ran cold" just that—a phrase. The chill along her veins proved it otherwise.

"You've had it," she snapped. "If you choose to disbelieve it, well, that's your little out, isn't it?"

"You have really not been with a man in over fourteen years?" Jared looked stunned.

As it was a truly honest question, Nacia answered it frankly. "No, I have really not been with a man in over fourteen years."

"But why?"

"Mostly because men disgust me, Mr. Ranklin. And at the moment, your name heads the list."

His lids narrowed over eyes alert to every nuance of her voice.

"Then," he murmured, "isn't it strange that you came so passionately alive beneath me?"

Nacia's bottom seemed to be glued to the seat. He *would* home in on the one point that had tormented her relentlessly through the dark hours.

"A purely physical reaction—completely contrary to my will." Though the reply was slow in forming, Nacia considered it an effective rebuttal.

"You don't really believe that!" Jared's tone held hard conviction. "You're so very obviously a strong-willed woman. That's a large part of your appeal." His ghost of a smile was rueful. "At least for me."

Pushing the plate with the half-eaten muffin away from her, Nacia glared at him defiantly. "You're implying a lot more than you're saying. Let's not tiptoe around. Spit it out."

"Right." The rueful smile vanished. "You set your will against mine the minute we met. Whether consciously or unconsciously, you issued a challenge. I merely accepted it."

"I see." Nacia's purring tone concealed the flash of anger that ripped through her. "Now comes the excuse."

"No excuse." The negative movement of his head was brief but sharp. "I began wanting you as I watched you walk through the sand to Frank. The wanting grew steadily until, when I entered your room, it was a very painful ache."

"And, of course, that gave you the right to—"

"I can truthfully say," he went on as if she had not even spoken, "that I have never before wanted any woman quite so badly. Not even my wife, and I loved her deeply.'' His dark-eyed gaze was compelling in its intensity. "Perhaps, had you not resisted, I'd have gone away satisfied with a good-night kiss or two.''

"Oh, spare me—'' Nacia began, but as before, he went on doggedly.

"Dammit, Nacia, why did you fight a simple kiss? Your resistance severed my control—and that's never happened before either.'' He shrugged fatalistically. "I didn't want to hurt you. I don't want to hurt you now. But make up your mind to it. I *am* going to have you.''

Shaken by the rock-hard finality of his tone, Nacia eyed him warily. She could feel the tension in him. It tugged at her as if trying to draw her into the vortex of his emotions. The sensation was downright scary. Somehow, she had to break free of the mesmerizing atmosphere he'd created around them.

"The next thing you know,'' she drawled with deliberate flippancy, "the man will be telling me he fell in love at first sight.''

"No.'' His smile was strangely, confusingly enigmatic. "The man won't be telling you that.''

For reasons Nacia couldn't begin to understand, Jared's assurance set off all kinds of warning signals. Like it or not, the time had definitely come to sound a retreat.

Moving abruptly, she slid out of the booth.

"Nacia?''

"Thank you for breakfast,'' she tossed over her shoulder as she headed for the door. Jared muttered something, but in her haste to escape, Nacia missed it.

The rain had slowed to a gentle sprinkle. As she strode purposefully toward her motel, Nacia noticed the stirring of life around her. The tires of several passing cars swished on the wet street, and one lone boy, his slim body protected by a yellow slicker, pedaled by on a beat-up ten-speed.

She should have heard him since there was no other pedestrian traffic. Possibly due to his sneakered feet, she didn't. Yet by the time she inserted the key in the lock on her motel room door, he was right behind her. His sudden appearance elicited a tiny shriek.

"Jared Ranklin! What is this thing you have for creeping up on me?" Not bothering to wait for a reply, she added, scathingly, "And what are you doing here, anyway?"

Unperturbed by her irritation, he lifted a hand that held a white paper bag. "You missed your second cup of coffee. I sprang for it."

His grin was contagious. Telling herself she was totally out of her mind, she allowed him entry into her room, her lips twitching in response.

"That's better." His grin widened into a smile. One of his front teeth had a small corner chip. "Don't be afraid of me, Nacia. I'll never take anything from you by force again."

Surprisingly, this time Nacia believed him. Against her common sense, she felt the worriness ease out of her. His smile was so genuinely warm, so enticing, she let the twitch in her own lips grow, if hesitatingly, to answer in kind.

"You could, and probably do, turn a man's head with that smile, honey," Jared murmured. "Come away from that temptingly rumpled bed and drink your coffee while it's still hot."

Embarrassment wiped the smile from her face. His soft laughter sent an unusual flush of color to her cheeks. Good grief! She hadn't blushed in years!

"I...I..." She had never stammered in her life! Pulling herself together, she bestowed a cool glance on him. "I guess it's a little early for the maid." Brilliant deduction! she chided herself.

Jared laughed outright. "Come drink your coffee, Nacia." Bending, he scooped the bedspread from the chair she'd flung it on before, and tossed it casually into a corner.

Lowering his long frame gingerly into the room's only other chair—a molded plastic contraption that made no pretense at comfort—he opened the bag and withdrew two foam cups.

While he was thus occupied, Nacia walked to the chair he'd cleared for her and sat down, repressing a shiver caused by her clammy T-shirt. When he handed one of the cups to her she took it gratefully, hoping to chase the chill with the hot liquid. As he handed it to her his fingers brushed hers and his gaze sharpened as he raked her body.

"Your hands are cold, and you're shivering." His concerned gaze probed hers. "Leave the coffee. Get out of those wet clothes."

Nacia bristled with fresh irritation at the note of command in his voice. Her movements deceptively relaxed, she slowly removed the opaque plastic lid and raised the cup to her lips.

"Okay, you've made your point." Jared again treated her to his disarming grin. "You don't appreciate being ordered around. I don't either." Placing his still-capped cup on the small table between the two chairs, he sprang lightly to his feet. "I'll make a deal with you. If you'll agree to change, I'll make myself scarce while you do it." Two long strides carried him to the door, where he paused to arch one dark, questioning brow at her. "Deal?"

"Yes." Recapping her cup, Nacia also rose.

Turning the doorknob, Jared opened the door, then shot an appraising look at her. "You will let me back in again?"

Casting him a pained expression, she nodded impatiently. "Yes, of course. Leave the door unlocked if you like." Swinging away from him confidently, she walked across the room and into the bathroom. Peeling her damp shirt and jeans from her goose bump-covered skin, Nacia eyed the shower stall longingly. When her underwear joined the sodden heap on the floor, she stood irresolute for mere seconds before giving in to the urge to step under the shiver-banishing warmth of a hot shower.

Four minutes later she stepped back onto the bath mat, her skin glowing and revitalized. A quick pat dry and she reached for her robe, a frown drawing her brows together when her fingernails scraped the door. The frown was directed at the hook on the door. Where was her robe?

Memory flashed, and she could see herself earlier that morning, carelessly dropping the garment onto the unmade bed.

"Damn."

The muttered sound bounced off the tiled walls Had Jared returned? Was he at that moment sprawled on that plastic excuse for a chair? A baffling curl of excitement unwound insidiously in her midsection.

Shocked by the anticipatory waves of heat washing over her, Nacia groaned softly.

What was happening to her? The question stabbed into her mind, not as with the pinprick of a needle, but more like the thrust of a broadsword. Was she actually standing here, wearing nothing but a blush, getting all hot and bothered at the mere thought of Jared Ranklin?

She was careening around the bend. There was simply no other explanation for her physical and emotional upheaval. It was so out of character as to be bizarre. Could it be a mid-life crisis?

Nacia grasped at the much-used excuse for irrational behavior with a degree of desperation. She *would* be thirty-six on her next birthday. Had she subconsciously been nurturing a fear of encroaching age? Did her emotional self crave the attention of a man to reaffirm her attractiveness as a woman? Could any of this self-analysis help her now—this minute?

Not likely. Nacia sighed with the realization that she still had to get from the bathroom to her robe. So much for in-depth thought, she chided herself, wrapping what now seemed a very skimpy towel around her nakedness. Feeling ridiculously like an insipid Victorian maiden, she clutched the edge of the towel with one hand and opened the door a crack with the other.

Home free! The room was blessedly empty.

Scurrying with an agility that would have put even Tracy to shame, Nacia dashed to the bed and scooped up the wrap. Dropping the towel, she thrust her arms into the full sleeves, then hastily tied the belt, only then releasing the breath she hadn't been aware of holding.

Now underwear. Two steps carried her to the desk-
like dresser. Yanking open the top drawer, she grasped
panties and bra. As she withdrew her hand, the door
to her room opened and Jared stepped inside, becoming still at the sight of her. It was impossible to deter-
mine which one of them was the more surprised.

Jared's startled expression changed to reveal masculine approval as his eyes traveled her length from her
bare feet to the disarrayed auburn mass of her hair.
When the dark gaze came to rest on the nylon and lace
clutched in her hand, a flicker acknowledged their
import.

In turn, Nacia's disbelieving stare was making a
minute perusal of him. How could it be? He'd been
gone at most ten minutes, yet he'd changed! Gone
were the cutoffs, jogging jacket and sneakers, replaced by tan cords, a terry cloth pullover in navy and
leather moccasins.

"You cheated." Jared's soft accusation scattered
her bemused thoughts. "The agreement was to
change. No one mentioned a shower."

"I was cold!" Taking him seriously, Nacia defended her actions heatedly.

"Hey, honey!" Jared held his hands up placat-
ingly, his eyes gleaming with laughter. "I was teasing." Bending to the small table, he flipped the lid off
one of the cups, then raised it to his lips. "Still warm,"
he pronounced. "Come over here and drink it."

"I— I have to get dressed."

Even as she made the protest Nacia walked to him
slowly, her hand outstretched for the cup he was now
holding out for her.

"Why?" His whisper tickled her nervous system from her ear to her heels. Raking her with a shadow-eyed glance, Jared drank deeply from his cup.

Suddenly parched, Nacia followed his actions, draining the tepid brew in a few seconds.

"Why am I convinced the coffee will not appease my thirst?" His gaze enmeshed with hers, Jared removed the foam container from her nerveless fingers and placed it and his own on the table.

"I *must* get dressed."

His head moving slowly from side to side, Jared closed in on her, his hands lifting to grasp the material of the robe's lapels.

"Jared?" The squeaky, breathless sound of her voice shook Nacia almost as much as her suddenly weakened knees. In effect, she literally stumbled into his arms.

"Why bother putting clothes on now?" His hands released the lapels to curl around her neck. "I'd only have to take them off again."

"No! Jared, you— Oh!" Nacia's breath lodged somewhere in the middle of her chest as his lips brushed over hers.

"You *are* going to let me kiss you this time?" The question seemed academic as, for all intents and purposes, he practically was kissing her. "You don't have to answer. All you have to do is open your mouth for me."

The mass of emotions raging inside Nacia threw her off-balance. It couldn't be that she wanted him to kiss her...could it? Her sudden need to experience the feel of his mouth didn't make sense—at least her kind of sense.

The deciding factor came not from her rational mind but from the glide of his hands down her spine. Sighing softly, Nacia parted her lips in invitation.

"Nacia."

The way he groaned her name sent a thrill racketing through her. The touch of his open mouth on hers set off an explosion. His hands retraced the path up her spine, molding her trembling, pliant body to the hardness of his own. At the nape his hands paused, long fingers kneading, soothing her tendons.

"You're all tight and trembly." Lifting his head, he gazed into her eyes, reading the confusion mirrored in them. "Are you remembering last night? The fear? The anger?" Not giving her time to answer, he slid his hands forward to cradle her face in his rough palms. "I don't know why you closed yourself off to men all these years, but I suspect your reasons are deep and painful."

"Jared—" Nacia had stiffened at his reference to the past. She didn't want to talk. She didn't want to remember. She wanted him to kiss her again.

"No." Mistaking her intent, his hands tightened, drawing her lips to within a hairbreadth of his. "I won't hurt you, darling." The gentleness of his tone caressed her as effectively as the brush of his lips to the corner of her mouth. "I want you. Every bit as badly as I did last night. But I won't—unless you want it too."

There was not an ounce of rejection left in Nacia's body. Moaning softly, she raised her arms to encircle his neck and fuse her mouth to his.

For one tiny instant he went still, as if with shocked disbelief; then he crushed her to him, his mouth feeding voraciously on the sweetness of hers.

Nacia's body, too long denied its natural release, burned in joyous expectation of coming delights. Her senses, too long suppressed, rioted with the slightest touch of his hands, the smallest movement of his body.

"Slowly, slowly."

In her bemusement Nacia had no idea if Jared's murmured caution was directed at her or himself. Her inhibitions submerged in the flow of sensuousness; she stole the initiative from him.

Spearing her fingers through his loose, springy curls, she drew his head closer to her own. Her darting tongue caressed his lips, then, at his groaning response, dipped inside the moist cavern of his mouth.

"God! Nacia, what are you trying to do?" His strangled tone had the effect of a bellows, fanning the flame licking through her veins.

"Trying?" Her purring query filled his mouth. "You mean I'm not succeeding?"

Jared nipped at her tongue. "Oh, you're succeeding all right." The hard tip of his tongue soothed the spot his teeth had touched. "If you're not careful, you're liable to find yourself being eaten alive!" To underline his threat he closed his teeth on her lower lip.

"All talk, no action." Nacia retaliated by trailing her nails down his back. "Are you cold?" Grasping the hem of his terry shirt, she gave an impatient tug. "Or do you need this for protection from me?"

His answer came in the form of swift, decisive action. The hands grasping her waist moved quickly to his shirt to pull it up his body and over his head. Before the terry cloth made contact with the carpet, his hands had reclaimed her waist.

"You want action, do you?" he growled tauntingly. "I'll give you so much action you'll think you've been through World War Three."

His hands came together between them, fingers worrying the knot in her sash. Reflecting his movements, Nacia set her fingers to work on his belt buckle.

As her fingers teased his smooth skin, he sucked in his breath, pulling in his already flat abdomen. "That does it!" he growled playfully.

His eyes gleaming almost black with arousal, Jared tore the sash open. Moving with maddening slowness, he separated the robe, his eyes examining every inch of her skin as it was revealed. By the time the robe slid off her arms onto the floor, his laughter was gone.

Breathing unevenly, he stepped back to view her with the intentness of a connoisseur of art viewing a masterwork.

Trembling and weak with a fourteen-year need clawing at her, Nacia watched him as he finished the task she'd begun on his buckle. She saw his legs move, then heard the thud as he kicked the moccasins from his feet. Her own breathing grew shallow as he unselfconsciously stepped out of his tan cords and flesh-toned briefs, and she held her breath altogether when he straightened to his full height.

In all truth he was a breathtaking sight! Unashamedly they stared at each other, each imprinting on their minds the other's likeness. As her eyes traveled slowly over him, Nacia's palms itched to follow the route. Naked, Jared had a lean, rangy look that was enhanced by the tightly knit muscles cording his shoulders, arms and chest. Her gaze, moving lower, appreciated the angular lines of slim hips blending into long straight legs. Even his feet were attractive. Her eyes climbed back up his legs and lingered, fascinated, on the proof of his manhood.

"Brazen woman."

Jared's taunt had more the sound of an endearment. Strangely elated, Nacia lifted her head to tangle her gaze with his.

"My husband was strictly a lights-out lover," she admitted starkly.

"And I'm the first male you ever—visually examined?"

Locked into his incredible navy blue gaze, Nacia nodded mutely in reply. Impossible as it seemed, it was true. Not once during their disastrous marriage had Nacia seen Clay stark naked; Clay had held the theory that a little mystery added spice to a marriage.

"Well?" Jared prompted. "What do you think?"

The incongruousness of the scene struck Nacia, and tickled her funny bone. Here they stood, as unadorned as the first couple: two fully mature adults, poles apart in their convictions—he the living definition of male supremacy, she a silent advocate of feminism—staring as avidly at each other's nakedness as two teenagers at their initiation into sex. The fact that they were in a motel room tickled her even more. An impish smile reflected her amusement.

"You think the male form is funny?" His stern tone was belied by the answering twitch of his lips. "Are you trying to annihilate my ego?"

The laughter trembling on Nacia's lips erupted. "Oh, Jared. It would take a million man-haters of Amazonian proportions to annihilate *your* ego."

"True."

Laughing with her, he reached out and drew her close to him. On contact, the banked embers of desire flared to roaring new life.

"Will you ever tell me what you really think?"

"Maybe." Giving in to temptation, she slid her hands up his chest. "Someday." Her fingertips skimmed over, then returned to tease his flat nipples. "If you're good."

"Oh, I'm good," Jared said, deliberately misinterpreting her. His hands slid around her rib cage, then up and over her breasts. At Nacia's tiny gasp of pleasure he bent close to her ear. "You see?" His teeth nipped at her earlobe. "With the right kind of encouragement, I'll be even better."

Long past the point of no return, Nacia encouraged him for all she was worth. She led him to the bed, and as he stretched out flat on his back, his devil-dark eyes issued a challenge to her. Kneeling beside him, she accepted it.

Like an intrepid explorer eager to make new discoveries, her hands charted the boundaries of his body, her lips tested the foreign terrain, her tongue tasted the fruits of the region.

Every inch of this new, masculine realm offered never before experienced delights—each one feeding the hungry flame of her own mounting sexual excitement.

Jared's deepening groans, the writhing of his steadily hardening body, goaded her on in her learning process. She was so lost in the quest, she failed to notice that his whispered, explicit words of excitement held a faint but distinct note of command.

"Come up here and kiss me," he gasped as she dipped her tongue into his navel.

Nacia took her time, dropping moist, tongue-tipped kisses from his midsection to his chin. When she feathered her lashes against his cheek, he grasped her face in his hands and brought her mouth to his.

"Are you trying to drive me crazy?" he muttered against her lips.

"Yes," she admitted throatily.

"You've succeeded." A light tug of his hands and their open mouths were joined.

The power of Jared's kiss shuddered through Nacia with the force of a sou'wester. Surprising her by suddenly taking the initiative, he heaved his body up and over, pinning her beneath him.

"Do you want to know the results of your endeavor?" he taunted hoarsely.

Staring into his passion-clouded eyes, Nacia whispered, "Yes."

"Say the words, Nacia." The control he was exerting over the urgings of his body was revealed in the lines of strain in his face, the harshness of his tone. "After last night I want to hear you say the words."

His body covered her from head to toe. Gently shifting her legs, Nacia formed a cradle for his body between her thighs.

"I want you, Jared." She gave him the words in a clear if soft tone. Reinforcing her admission, she arched her hips in a silent invitation. "Please."

It was not exactly clear who surrendered to whom.

In the stillness of the room, Jared listened to the sound of his own breathing returning to a more even, normal rate. Lying beside him, exhausted from the violence of total release, the woman he would now die or kill for slept trustingly within the safety of his embrace.

Lord, she was magnificent! He couldn't let her go—not now, not ever! But how to keep her?

The thought sent a fearful command from his mind to his arms, tightening them compulsively. Exerting mind over matter, Jared loosened his hold fractionally. Be careful, you fool, don't frighten her! She has surrendered her body to you—not her trust. Moving slowly, he turned his head to place his lips to her temple. The clean scent of her hair filled his senses; the satiny softness of her skin was arousing, surprising him into stillness. Was it really possible? Apparently so, for he wanted her again, the urgency almost as sharp as it had been before. How many years had it been since he'd known this kind of passion? More than he cared to count. He was pushing forty-two. Hell, he didn't *expect* flaming desire twice in as many hours! As a matter of fact, until recently, he hadn't been able to get too excited about any female. In truth, the near dormant state of his sexual life had not bothered him all that much. He had merely put it down to physical weariness due to overwork. Yet here he was, every bit as tired if not more so, and hotter than a nineteen-year-old who'd been incarcerated for over a year! Her skin was so soft!

Jared's lips moved slowly across her face, while his hands sought the silkiness of her thigh. She moaned softly, encouragingly, in her sleep, driving the flame higher, his lips lower.

Chapter 5

Nacia found it difficult to sleep with lips tugging, even gently, on a vulnerable part of her anatomy.

Forcing sleep-heavy eyelids apart, Nacia glanced down at the tousled head at her breast.

"Dinnertime already?" she drawled, then gasped aloud as his teeth extracted revenge.

"Smart-mouthed broad." His flicking tongue lashed her sensuously.

"Broad?" Filling her hands with curls, she jerked his head up. "Broad?" she repeated in not altogether feigned indignation. Glaring into his laughing dark eyes, Nacia asked herself why she should be even mildly shocked or, more unsettling, hurt. She knew, had known on first meeting, what type of man he was. But she was shocked and hurt, and she resented his ability to arouse either emotion in her.

"Dismount."

Nacia blinked at his whispered advice, thereby losing the effectiveness of her fierce stare.

"What?"

"Step down off that high horse," he soothed, repressing the amusement reflected in his eyes. "I meant nothing derogatory by the term." Shifting his body, he placed his forearms on either side of her shoulders, then deliberately lowered his chest to crush her breasts beneath him. "In my personal estimation, all strong-willed, independent women are tough broads." He brought his mouth close to hers and she felt his warm breath caress her lips. "I like tough broads."

Of course, he would! The unpalatable realization had to be faced. What sense of achievement could there be for him in mastering a weak, too willing ninny? Nacia tried to ignore the deepening hurt. It was like trying to ignore a blade handle sticking out of her chest. At any rate, when it had come down to the crunch, how tough *had* she been?

"You lied to me."

Her eyes sprang wide again.

"I never lie!" Stung by something in his tone, Nacia's denial came swiftly, angrily.

"No?" Jared's eyes assessed her expression. "Then what was all that business about not having been with a man in fourteen years?"

Suddenly incensed, both with him and with herself, Nacia brought her hands to his shoulders and pushed at him ineffectively. "That business was the truth," she hissed. "Why would I lie about that?"

"To impress me?" Jared's lips turned up at the corners in a suspiciously self-satisfied smile, agitating Nacia further.

"You—you—" Nacia sputtered, at a loss for words. "You were the last man I would have wanted to impress! Why did you think I—" His mouth silenced her.

Annoyed, Nacia struggled against him, first pushing at his chest, then pulling at his hair. The battle was short-lived as all the fight drained out of her at the first thrust of his foraging tongue.

Soft inarticulate murmurs vibrating her throat, Nacia speared her fingers through his loose curls and pulled him closer still.

When she was finally pliant in his arms, he lifted his head to stare down at her, his expression stern.

"I thought you lied because of the way you made love to me," he rasped unevenly. At her gasp of protest, he dipped his head to plant a swift hard kiss on her parted lips. "You *did* make love to me. Very expertly, too." In the dimly lighted room, his teeth were a flash of white when he grinned. "It was very exciting and I loved every minute of it. Your seeming...ah, expertise created the doubt, but it wouldn't have mattered either way. Whether or not there have been other men is unimportant. It's the here and now that's important." The grin dissolved, to be replaced by a smile so sensuous that a thrill of expectation drove the breath from Nacia's chest. "And right here, right now, it's my turn to make love to you."

"Jared, no, I—"

"Shut up, Nacia." His soft tone robbed the order of its sting. "Just relax and enjoy." His lips moved in an erratic line across her cheek. "I promise you, you will." With his last word, his tongue slid into the hollow behind her earlobe, and all thoughts of protest flew out of Nacia's head.

Jared kept his promise with gentle, exquisite thoroughness. His hands and lips moving with breath-stopping laziness, he searched out, and claimed as his own, every tiny, sensitive spot.

By the time he slid suggestively up the length of her body, Nacia was consumed by a hunger only he could assuage. At that moment nothing, not the differences between them, not her job or other responsibilities, *nothing* else mattered. Whimpering, she clung to Jared, her every movement begging him to free her from the maelstrom of swirling sensations.

When, at long last, Jared shattered the invisible cage of her tension, her soaring flight led, for infinitesimal moments, into the waiting arms of unconsciousness.

Her softness cushioning the weight of Jared's spent body, Nacia lay perfectly still, her now alert intellect marshaling arguments against the magnitude of the experience, attempting to assure itself that the everything of the physical act meant nothing.

As his breathing returned to a more normal rate, Jared raised his head from her pillowing shoulder to stare deeply into her eyes.

The eyes are the window of the soul. The phrase swirled into her mind. Staring back at him, Nacia decided that if the phrase had any validity, at the moment Jared's soul was at peace. The depths of his beautiful blue eyes were as placid and unruffled as a mountain lake.

Murmuring a sigh of satisfaction, Jared carefully slid his long frame onto the mattress beside her, his enjoyment of the feel of his hair-roughened skin against her smoothness made obvious by the very slowness of his movement. Gathering her close, he settled her against the side of his chest and buried his face in her tangled auburn hair.

"Your hair smells good." His warm breath whispered through the tangled strands. "Like—" He hesitated, as if trying to pinpoint the exact words. "Like the tantalizing, elusive scent that rides on the first warm breezes of spring."

Moving slowly, his hand stroked down her side from her underarm to her thigh. "Your skin has the texture of warm satin." The observation was breathed huskily near her temple as his lips began an exploration of their own. Flat-palmed, his fingers splayed, his caressing hand teased the supple roundness of her buttocks. "Full and firm," he approved. "Exactly as a mature woman should be." He sighed. "I'm disappointed."

Bemused by the silkiness of his touch and his compliments, several seconds elapsed before his gibe penetrated.

"Disappointed?" Nacia's confused gaze met his. "In what way are you disappointed?" Nacia was amazed at the helpless, inadequate feeling that washed over her. She had thought, and he had indicated, that he had derived every bit as much satisfaction from their union as she. Having him bluntly tell her she'd disappointed him... She clenched her teeth in an effort to suppress a shiver born of a sense of rejection.

Jared's response to her shiver was immediate. "Are you cold?" Not waiting for an answer, he stretched one long arm out to grasp a corner of the blanket, tugging it up and over the both of them. "Better?"

Shifting slightly, he settled her more closely to his warmth.

"Why are you disappointed?" The quivering sound of her voice amazed her almost as much as the feeling of inadequacy.

"Hmmm..." Jared's stroking hand was on the move again, making a slow run down her thigh. "Oh, that." Lifting his lips from the outside point of her eyebrow, he gazed at her with teasing eyes. "I'm disappointed in your laziness." At her frown, he elaborated. "You know, in sex games, the play should be reciprocal both before and after." His fingers trailed up her leg; then, beginning to measure the distance between her hipbones, they made an unscheduled stop halfway along the route, trekking downward. "Like silk," he husked, combing through the tight curls.

"Oh!" Nacia gasped softly, whether from his tantalizing fingers or his chiding tutelage she didn't know, or really care. "Now I get it. You want to be stroked like a big ole tomcat?"

His soft laughter was a delight to her ears. "Of course." His tone said it should have been obvious.

It wasn't. At least not to Nacia. Clay had never bothered to touch her after they made love. He always headed straight for the shower as if he were ashamed of the perspiration his physical activity had wrought. Come to that, there had been precious little foreplay either. Jared's brand of play was a revelation—a very enjoyable revelation. "Do you expect compliments as well?" Even as she posed the question, she laid her palm on his chest.

"Certainly." Jared's answer came quickly, adamantly. "I'm a greedy tomcat. I'm looking forward to having my ego stroked along with my hide." He went still when she slid her hand over his flat nipple, and shivered with pleasure when she touched an examining fingertip to it.

"It feels funny," she offered, lips twitching.

"Some compliment." Jared's growl failed in its attempt at masking his amusement. "You'll have to do better than that."

"You're bony," she teased, poking a rib.

"But tough," he countered.

"Your skin's not tough." Nacia's tone lost its taunt as she wondered at the smoothness of him. "It's remarkably sleek, soft to the touch."

"You're improving." He rewarded her with a tiny kiss to the corner of her mouth.

Gliding up, her hand roamed over his chest to his shoulders. "Definitely not bony here. Do you work out? Lifting weights?" He moved his head in the negative. "Not muscle-bound," she approved. "Just muscular. I like the feel of the long cord, as opposed to the bulge."

"Better and better." This time her reward came in the form of teeth nibbling gently on her earlobe.

Her hand wove an erratic path down his arm to his hand, her touch probing the soft areas between his fingers.

"The texture of the skin on your forearm is different. Exposure to the elements has toughened it, made it leathery."

"Like an old pair of boots?"

Ignoring his comment, Nacia, absorbed now with this new, exciting learning experience, continued categorizing. "There's a great deal of strength in your fingers. You're not a stranger to hard work."

The hand under discussion closed around hers in a brief squeeze. "It's apparent you're a novice at this game. I think I'll have to broaden your adjective vocabulary."

"You want flowery praise?" Nacia's taunt held more than a hint of surprise.

"Of course." Jared's emphatic concurrence surprised her even more—possibly because Clay had always tightened up at what he'd termed sweet talk. Now here was another man practically demanding it. The fact that her ex-husband had, at the time, only recently emerged from adolescence, while Jared was a fully mature man, didn't penetrate the sensuous fog clouding her mind.

"Having strength does not preclude the need for approval," he instructed softly. "A man, an *honest* man, will admit to longing to hear a soft, feminine voice extol his attributes, even if he possesses very few." He laughed softly. "She can always lie."

"You smell good."

Jared's laughter deepened. "Now I'm suspicious."

"But you *do* smell good," she insisted. "Sandalwood?"

"Yes." Jared made an obvious effort at controlling his mirth.

"In combination with your—ah—more earthy male scent, it's very potent, very sexy."

"That was the general idea." Jared's laughter escaped his control. His arms releasing her, he flung them wide, his body undulating as he stretched contentedly. His sudden, vigorous action dislodged the blanket, and with a final thrust of his long legs he kicked it away.

"The results are worth the extra splash I slapped on." Tilting his head, he slanted a devilish look at her. "I wonder what would happen if I took a bath in the stuff?"

"Instant sterility?" Nacia teased dryly.

Jared's reaction stunned her. His teeth gleamed through a beginning grin; then suddenly, his smile fell apart and he grew rigidly still.

"Jared, I was only kid—"

He silenced her by groaning aloud before heaving himself off the bed to prowl restlessly around the room, totally unconcerned with his nakedness, a dark scowl on his face.

"Jared, what—?"

"Damn," Jared swore, interrupting her question. His fierce look sent a quiver of anxiety through her. He was standing in front of the desk lamp that she had switched on early that morning, his expression in shadow, but the still tautness of his stance was chilling.

"Is there no end to my stupidity?" he bit out angrily.

"Jared." Her nerves tight, Nacia drew out his name.

"As if it wasn't enough that I began by manhandling you, I put you in jeopardy three times," he breathed in self-anger, then repeated, "*three* times."

Confused, exasperated, Nacia bolted to a sitting position, unmindful of the fact that she was also naked.

"What *are* you talking about?" she demanded.

"Are you on the pill?" he shot back roughly.

"Of course not!"

"Of course not," he echoed softly. "You had no reason to take it. And that's what I'm talking about. I used no precautions." His broad, curly-haired chest expanded with his deep sigh. "Nacia, what if I've made you pregnant?"

The light had dawned in Nacia before his final question. Her teeth worrying her lower lip, she stared at him, her mind shying away from defining the cause of the jerk of excitement in her stomach. Rather than contemplate the unthinkable, her mind settled on the cause of his concern. What would she do? What *could* she do, other than the obvious? But the whole idea was too ludicrous, not worth serious consideration. Reassured, she permitted a taunting note to enter her tone, and a fatalistic shrug to lift her shoulders.

"I suppose you'll first have to marry me," she taunted facetiously.

Turning slightly, he tilted his head in a pose of consideration. His move allowed the soft glow of light to play over his features. Nacia found it impossible to interpret his odd expression.

"Maybe we ought to play it safe," he said slowly, "and get married now."

"You *are* crazy!" Nacia exclaimed.

"Why?"

Shaken far more than she cared to admit, even to herself, Nacia took refuge in ridicule.

"Because that's the craziest thing I've heard in months. I'm certainly not getting married on the off chance of having conceived! Come to that, I'm not sure I'd want to get married if I *knew* I'd conceived."

"Really?" His tone mocked her.

"Really." Her tone was adamant.

"Whatever you say." Jared's shrug was almost too casual. "You're the boss, after all."

"And you're studying to be a stand-up comedian?" Nacia tossed the gibe nastily, perversely nettled by his easy acceptance of her refusal.

Her cool front was firmly in place. Not for the world would she reveal to him the germ of doubt incubating in her mind. With the clarity of hindsight she remembered the twinges of pain in her side that she had ignored in the office Friday afternoon. Oh, damn, what would she do if...

"I guess we'll have to hold our breath for a few weeks...." Jared's musing tone scattered her thoughts. "But from now on I'm going to be very careful of you in that respect."

Nacia was already holding her breath, but not for the reason he'd mentioned.

From now on. The phrase skipped back and forth through her head. Was there to be a from now on? The realization that she had not thought beyond the moment sent a ripple of shock through her. Not to think ahead was simply not like her; she always thought ahead, not only of the next hours but of the coming weeks and months! That she had abandoned all rational thought because of this man deepened the shock alarmingly.

"Are you comatose?"

Nacia blinked, only then becoming aware that she had been staring at him, yet not seeing him. That fact alone said much about her rattled state, for he was certainly something to see. In the throes of passion her hands had learned all there was to know of his body. Now her gaze absorbed the impact of his male beauty.

He was not, by any stretch of the imagination, brawny. Every deeply tanned inch of his six-foot-plus, sinewy frame projected a deceptive image of slenderness; even his feet were narrow.

Nacia had been clasped within the confines of his embrace, had become a part of him by the act of physical possession; she knew the power in that lean form. Her gaze halted, lingering on the strongest yet most vulnerable part of his anatomy.

"Stop it, Nacia." Jared's laughing order drew her eyes to him. "I'm hungry."

Her gaze dropped, then returned to his face to confront the teasing light in the navy depths. "I see," she drawled, suddenly dry mouthed.

"For food, wanton!" His pretense of shock didn't quite hide the thread of excitement woven through his tone. "Do you realize how long it's been since I've eaten?"

The growing excitement in him, evident now both vocally and visually, ignited a like response in her. Tossing the last of her inhibitions aside, Nacia moved her body in sensuous invitation.

"Oh, yes, I know," she whispered throatily. "But do you realize how long it's been since you made love to me?"

Jared was electrified. For one brief instant he stood statue still; then, a rumbling bark of laughter erupting from his throat, he leaped onto the bed, gathering her into his arms in a fierce bear hug.

"God, you are one fantastic woman." His momentum carried him onto his back, and he grinned up at her. "The fact that you're my woman instills the urge in me to crow like a strutting rooster." One dark brow arched suggestively. "Want to see me preen my feathers?"

His mood was infectious. Laughing softly, Nacia tugged at a dark curl on his chest. "Your 'feathers' reveal what an old bird you really are. There are a few gray amongst the brown." Her finely arched brow reflected his action. "Are you sure you can still cock-a-doodle-do?"

"That's positively fowl!" Jared cried indignantly, smirking at her pained expression. Unlocking his bone-crushing hold, he raised his hands to clasp her face and draw her lips close to his own.

"I may be pushing forty-two, boss lady, but I'm sure as hell still capable of cock-a-doodling *your* do."

Some two hours later, her mind still bemused by the experience of making love while laughing all the way, Nacia studied the relaxed visage of the man sitting across the table from her.

At three o'clock on a dreary gray Sunday afternoon, the small restaurant was empty except for herself and Jared, and a family of four seated on the other side of the room.

Her bemusement finally dissolving, Nacia shifted her mental gears from Jared's attractive face to her own precarious position. Faithful to his stated word, he had taken a second just before the culmination of their rather giddy passion play to insure her protection. Her throat tight, she wondered if that final, somewhat hilarious encounter had been the extent of his "from now on." And was this really Nacia Barns? Was she actually making herself half sick over the prospect of *not* seeing a man who was the prototype of all she abhorred in the male of the species?

Nacia forced herself to face the realization that while this infatuation lasted, she wanted nothing more than to lose herself inside the hot, sensuous world only *he* seemed capable of creating around her.

Madness indeed!

Feeling the intentness of her regard, Jared paused in his evident enjoyment of the bowl of clam chowder before him to fix her with a contemplative stare.

"Why do I get this uncomfortable feeling I'm being dissected?" he wondered aloud teasingly before his tone went low with seriousness. "What's on your mind, Nacia?"

Nacia shook her head dismissingly. "It'll wait. Finish your soup."

Slicing brooding glances at her, he emptied the bowl, then pushed it to the side. "Now—" He paused as the waiter appeared at their table to remove his bowl and place a large Greek salad in front of Nacia and a steak sandwich before him.

"Now," he repeated as the waiter departed. "What?"

Nacia had never been one to dissemble; she didn't now. "I was wondering where we go from here."

Jared chose to misunderstand. "We could go to one of the casinos and gamble for a couple of hours."

In the process of breaking a two-inch square of feta cheese into bite-size chunks, Nacia glanced up sharply, her fork quivering in midair over the salad. "That's not what I mean and you know it."

"Yeah." His smile was apologetic. "Okay, where do we go from here?"

"I—" Nacia shrugged. "We're not exactly—"

"Suited?" Jared finished for her. "I know. The man-hater and the—" He smiled. "Neanderthal with a macho mentality."

"Jared."

"But we're good together." Again he interrupted. "Very good. And I know you get as much pleasure from my body as I get from yours." His smile widened as she looked around quickly to assure herself he hadn't been overheard. "I don't want that pleasure to end." Her gaze shot back to his, and he added, "Just yet. And, if you're honest, you'll admit you're not ready to have it end yet either." His brows arched questioningly. "Are you?"

Nacia went back to jabbing at the cheese, but she shook her head. "No."

The sigh that whispered through his lips betrayed the breath he'd been holding. "Then the only question is, what arrangements do we make?"

That brought her eyes back to his. "I don't know." She frowned, admitting, "I'm unfamiliar with this kind of thing. What do you suggest?"

"Assuming, of course, that I am familiar with 'this kind of thing,'" he drawled.

"I didn't say that!" Nacia bristled, simply because she *had* made the assumption.

His smile was pitying. "You didn't have to say it aloud." Before she could protest he shook his head. "No matter," he insisted smoothly. "Let's get back to the point. I heard you tell Frank you're on vacation." At her nod, he asked, "For how long?"

"Two weeks."

"You have your motel room booked for that long?"

"No, they could only give me a week."

"And my tenancy runs out tomorrow morning," he supplied.

Nacia was jolted with the realization of how little she knew about him. Madness! Even as she thought the word, she probed, "Where are you staying?"

Now his smile had a sardonic twist. "In a room on the floor below yours."

No wonder he'd been able to change clothes so quickly earlier that morning! Feeling like a fool, Nacia glared at him. Jared managed to look innocent.

"You didn't ask." He shrugged his shoulders. "But, we're digressing. I suggest I move in with you for the remainder of your stay. After that, we'll play it by ear. Okay?"

The words "move in with you" brought home to Nacia exactly what she was getting into here, and she hesitated, uncertain.

"Nacia?"

"I—" She wet her lips. "I suppose so."

"No." Nacia started at the harshness of his tone. "You don't suppose. You're either sure you want to be with me, or you're not *going* to be with me."

"For how long?" she rasped, goaded into irritation.

Jared's eyes drifted over her with cool insolence. "Until we're satiated," he stated bluntly. "What's it going to be? Yes or no?"

Damn it! Damn him! Nacia sighed. And curse this sudden, inexplicable physical need that demanded satisfaction. Nacia had not tasted defeat this bitter since divorcing Clay. She swallowed with difficulty, but faced him fearlessly.

"Yes."

"Good girl."

His praise was murmured so softly Nacia wasn't sure she'd heard him correctly. Denying the glow of pleasure she felt, she attacked her salad.

By the time they left the restaurant, Nacia was so tense her neck was stiff and achy. Walking back to the motel, she forced herself to breathe slowly, deeply, an exercise that proved difficult as she had to stride briskly to keep up with Jared's long steps.

As they neared the motel a fine film of perspiration sheened her face and her stomach began a growling protest against her hastily consumed lunch. With each successive step the prospect of what she was about to do tightened nerves already at the quiver stage.

Jared spoke for the first time as they passed through the motel entrance, and it took every ounce of control Nacia possessed to control a humiliating flinch.

"You go on up," he directed quietly. "I'll collect my gear and follow you."

"Oh, but you said your room is paid for through tonight!" Her control was slipping, and her voice cracked.

"What difference does that make?" he snapped impatiently, thereby revealing his own tension. "I thought the idea was for us to be together?"

"I know, I know...but..." Nacia faltered at his narrow-eyed examination of her.

"There's always a but," he mimicked her gibe of earlier that morning. "Okay, Nacia," he sighed. "I'll wait until tomorrow morning to lug my stuff up to your room." Cocking his head, he smiled ruefully. "So, what do you want to do?"

With her eyelids beginning to feel gritty from lack of sleep, Nacia was prompt with her answer. "Take a nap."

Jared's expression brightened. "Excellent idea."

"Alone."

"Sorehead."

"The idea was to sleep." Nacia was hard put not to laugh at his dramatically woeful expression. "And besides that, I told my daughter I'd call her between four and five this afternoon."

"You win—one more time." The look of him warned her there would not be many more times. Lifting his wrist, he shot a glance at his watch. "It's just past four now. How does seven-thirty sound for dinner?"

"I'll be ready."

Nacia turned to the stairs only to be brought to a stop by his hand grasping her shoulder. Frowning in confusion, she looked up sharply to find his face close to hers.

"A little something on deposit," he murmured. His hard kiss was over quickly, but memorable just the same. "I'll give you the balance later."

If there was one thing that always made Nacia uncomfortable it was a public display of affection. Not that she had ever indulged in it. But simply being an observer made her uncomfortable. Now, being a recipient, she found that although she'd enjoyed his kiss, she was embarrassed. Spinning away from him, she ran up the steps and along the concrete walkway. Safely inside her room, the door locked behind her, Nacia sagged as the tension eased out of her taut body.

Without giving herself time to think, she drew her address book from her handbag and, after committing the Florida number to memory, lifted the receiver and punched out the number. The hotel operator in Florida answered on the third ring and within seconds was ringing the room number Nacia had requested.

"Hello?" Tracy answered on the second ring.

"Hi, honey. How's Florida?"

"Hi, Mom! It's great. You'd hate it. It's hot as you-know-what." Tracy's laughing enthusiasm rang a sane note in Nacia's self-created insanity.

Shaken with the sudden weird sensation that she had split into two different and distinct personalities, Nacia strove for a near-normal drawl.

"I hate to say I told you so, but I told you so." Unfamiliar tears clouded her eyes as she pictured her daughter's alert, grinning face. "Are you having a good time, honey?" Nacia had known the answer, yet she had to ask.

"Great." Tracy's laughter hurt Nacia's ears, and her heart. "The look-alikes are a riot," she confided, referring to her twin half sisters. "They've got more bounce than basketballs. And the really terrific part is, the place isn't packed. We've hardly had to wait in any lines at all." Used to Tracy's quick change in topics, Nacia merely smiled as the girl paused to gulp a fortifying breath. "We just got back to the room right before you called. We were having the once-a-day rain shower, so we came back to clean up for dinner."

Nacia could hear the murmur of voices in the background, so she asked the obvious. "I hear voices. Is everyone in your room?"

"No, just Dilly and Dally." A burst of giggles greeted Tracy's answer, informing Nacia that the twins were anything but displeased with their nicknames. "We're sharing one room," Tracy went on, "and Dad and Gloria are in the connecting room."

How convenient for Clay and Gloria—a vacation with a built-in baby-sitter. Even as the condemnation flashed through her mind, Nacia decided she was judging too harshly. But, hell, she'd never had any vacation time away from Tracy in all the years she was growing up. Not until now, and *now* was beginning to get scary. Meanwhile, Tracy was chattering on, something about one of the twins having remarked "I hope it keeps up" about the rain shower.

"Do you get it, Mom? She hopes it keeps *up.*"

"Yes, Tracy, I do get it." Nacia smiled, enjoying the child's joke simply because Tracy did. "Honey, I'd like to talk to your father, if he's close by."

"Yeah, sure, hang on and I'll get him."

The voice that answered did not belong to Clay Barns.

"Nacia? This is Gloria. Clay is in the shower." Gloria's voice was warm, if a little strained, which made Nacia wonder if Clay had described her as some sort of ogre. "Can I help you?"

Having given in to a devil urge to sink a small barb into Clay about taking Tracy with him to baby-sit, Nacia had to rack her mind for something to say.

"Yes, of course, Gloria." She infused her tone with a warmth to match the other woman's. "I just wanted to caution Clay about riding herd on Tracy when she's in the water. She tends to get a little overenthusiastic."

"Clay is being very careful with all three of his daughters, Nacia."

Nacia knew the mild sting in Gloria's tone was a definite slap. In all honesty, she had to admit she deserved a put-down.

"I'm relieved." What else could she say? Feeling very much like the shrew Clay insisted she was, Nacia asked if she could speak to Tracy again.

Tracy rattled on for another ten minutes. When Nacia replaced the receiver, she had to blink furiously against a fresh onslaught of tears.

What was the matter with her? She never cried! Was this another sign of mid-life crisis?

Positive she wouldn't sleep, Nacia nonetheless called the desk to request a wake-up call at six forty-five; then, dropping her clothes carelessly to the floor as she removed them, she slid between the still-rumpled sheets.

At seven-fifteen, refreshed from the nap and a reviving shower, Nacia stood at the bathroom mirror applying makeup carefully to her face while giving a stern if silent lecture to her reflection.

You are thirty-five years old, my girl. She blinked as a smidgen of mascara found its way into her eye. You have been without the company of a man for the majority of those thirty-five years. Yet now, for no apparent or sensible reason, you become all hot, bothered and weak in the knees every time a man touches you. She frowned at herself.

All right, she continued her lecture, granted, you don't fall apart when just any man touches you, but when *that* man touches you.

Nacia frowned back.

You've got an excellent job. No, you don't have a job, you have a position. You have a condominium that is, if not quite posh, practically luxurious. You have a wonderful, well-behaved, loving daughter. You do what you please, when you please. The last thing you need is a domineering, tormenting, muscle-flexing man.

But I want him, she told herself defiantly.

Turning away from the mirror, Nacia walked out of the bedroom. While she finished dressing she came to terms with her delayed—much delayed—awakening libido. Whoever heard of a sleeping libido? She hadn't even been taking vitamins.

So indulge yourself; let the urge run its course. It probably won't take very long until, as he'd put it, they were both satiated. When it's over, put it down as a learning experience and go about the *real* business of your life.

Satisfied with her rationalization of the situation, Nacia smiled at her reflection in the dresser mirror and fluffed the ruffle around the deep V neckline of her sheer, muted pink-and-beige dress.

Jared knocked on the door at exactly seven-thirty. Her smile still in place, she opened the door and stepped back. As he entered the room he eyed her speculatively.

"Have you been drinking?" he teased.

Nacia laughed and, walking to him, slid her arms around his waist. "No."

"Then what do I have to thank for this reception?" His smile set off a flood of excitement in her veins that she made no attempt to curb. "The last I saw of you, you were running away from me."

"I've been soul-searching," Nacia confessed.

"And?"

In a move designed to brush the tips of her breasts against his chest, she shrugged with the entire top half of her body.

"I decided to stop running."

Very quietly, Jared let the constricted air ease slowly, carefully out of his tortured lungs. Although she had agreed to spend the week with him, until this moment the fear that she would change her mind had nagged at him incessantly.

The minute she had swung away from him down in the lobby, so very obviously embarrassed by his kiss, he had felt the pressure beginning to build inside his chest.

Pacing his room, one thought had circled endlessly around in his head: What would he do if she changed her mind? Oh, the realization was there on the fringes of his consciousness that he was not behaving in a very rational way; but then, he wasn't feeling very rational at this moment!

Not only had Jared resisted the arms of Morpheus, he hadn't sat down for longer than three minutes at a time. Jared was not by nature a high-strung or nervous person. Most of his friends described him as exceedingly laid-back. Anxiety was not his thing, yet he had prowled his small room like a death row inmate waiting for an eleventh-hour call from the governor.

As he dressed casually but carefully in dark brown slacks, a stark white-and-brown striped shirt, and fawn-colored sport coat Jared had assured himself that he would calmly abide by her decision, no matter what that decision happened to be. By the time he had traversed the short distance between his room and hers, each successive breath he drew in had become an ordeal.

Now, with her breasts brushing provocatively against him, Jared smiled and silently repeated those five beautiful words: I decided to stop running.

Chapter 6

There are moments in life, precious and rare, that give buoyancy to the spirit. The duration of these moments is as unpredictable as the moments themselves.

For Nacia, perhaps because these moments had been extremely rare, the joy lasted for over a week. Because she'd never experienced a candlelight, champagne dinner, and a companion who practically devoured her with his eyes, she was all the more susceptible to the romantic mood.

In other words, she was a pushover.

Her disdain of the opposite sex, her rigidly held moral principles, even her previous single-minded concentration on her job, all fell by the wayside when it came to Jared. To Nacia, he posed an enigmatic problem. Unused to being confused about anything, she was thrown off her mental stride. Despite his indolent appearance on their first encounter, Nacia had recognized the essence of indomitable male in him. The first night they'd spent together seemed to prove her estimation of him correct. But ever since their walk on the beach the morning after their stormy lovemaking, he had presented a contradiction that teased her normally rational mind.

When she was expecting arrogance, he displayed humility. Looking for a show of supreme confidence, she found a hint of uncertainty. Waiting for him to reveal cool disregard, he confounded her with tender consideration. One by one he shot all of her preconceived notions to smithereens.

Not that she learned much about him that week; she didn't. Nor did he learn much about her. Except in a purely physical sense.

They spent the majority of that week between the sheets.

"You're a fantastic lover," Nacia was compelled to compliment him after one earth-moving episode early Monday morning.

"In comparison to whom?" Jared teased.

In fact, Jared teased her incessantly—with his words, with his lips, with his tongue, with his hands and, most exciting of all, with his entire body.

Having given in to abandonment, Nacia wallowed in it. She was on vacation, wasn't she? Vacations were taken for the purpose of relaxing, weren't they? Well, she was relaxed to a state of near bonelessness—not to mention brainlessness.

Gone were all the inhibitions she'd ever harbored, and they were legion. When one vacationed in the land of sensuality, one left one's maidenly blushes at home.

Jared's total lack of self-consciousness convinced Nacia of his familiarity with the resort of the senses.

Unlike the men she'd heard of from friends and relatives, Jared evinced not the slightest difficulty in forming words of endearment. Indeed, Nacia was hard put to think of one he did not use at least once during that week.

It was:

"Darling, would you like more wine?"

Or:

"Honey, come scrub my back."

Once:

"You look sexy as hell in that dress, sweetheart."

Even:

"Stay in bed this morning, dearest; I'll go get us a take-out breakfast at McDonalds."

And quite often:

"Yes, my love, touch me there, and there, and...oh, God... *there.*"

As the moments of that week spun out, they gambled at the casino, they played together, they ate, they slept—never once probing into each other's private lives. It was too precious, too rare; it couldn't last and it didn't. Reality intruded in the form of curiosity late Friday afternoon.

"What went wrong with your marriage, hon?"

Nacia was sitting at the desk-dresser applying a coat of coppery-toned enamel to her nails. The mildly spoken, innocent-sounding query sent a tremor along her arms and she painted her cuticle.

Frowning at her nail, she carefully cleaned the polish from her skin before glancing up at him.

"Why?"

Jared was stretched out on the bed, his back propped against the headboard, the paper he had been reading tossed to one side. At the sharpness of her tone, his eyebrows arched in surprise. "Why what?"

A cold feeling of foreboding blanketed the tremor that shook Nacia. The illusion was shattered, exposing her conscience to the truth of their situation. They were having an affair. A common, garden variety affair. A physical attraction that, certainly unimpeded by her, had culminated in the sex act, over, and over, and over.

The chill permeating her entire being, Nacia let her gaze travel the slender length of him slowly before raising her eyes to his now frowning face.

"Nacia?" Jared's steady tone failed to mask the concern in his voice. "I asked you a question."

Nacia was certain that it was the first of many. "Why are you prying now?" she countered, finally finding her voice.

"Prying?" His expression incredulous, Jared sat up straight. "Prying?" he repeated as if unable to believe he'd heard correctly. "What the hell are you saying? You consider the fact that I'm interested in all the aspects of your life as prying? Good God, woman! I would think you'd be as interested in my life." His eyes bored into hers.

Was she interested in learning more than the physical side of him? Of course she was. Hadn't she been mentally dodging the need to know for the better part of a week? The realization frightened her. She didn't want to experience that need. The last time she'd allowed herself—

"Say something, Nacia!"

Nacia blinked at his harsh tone. He was angry, and getting angrier with every second she remained silent.

"What do you want to know?" Somehow she'd managed to keep her voice cool.

"Everything." A gentle smile softened his bluntness. "I already know your body. Now I want to know your mind."

"We have to be out of this room by eleven tomorrow morning," she observed dryly, hoping to deflect his interrogation. "Hardly enough time for any in-depth questioning."

Jared moved his body to the edge of the bed closest to her. "I hadn't forgotten, darling." His grin left her wondering if he was wise to her tactics. "Okay, we'll shelve the 'in-depth' discussion until after we've relocated. Which brings up a question on a different subject. Where would you like to go from here? One of the casino hotels? Someplace else along the coast? Europe? South America? The Ukraine? My place?" The last was accompanied by a definite leer.

"Your place."

If her answer surprised him—and from his startled expression it obviously had—it shocked her, too. Where in blue blazes had the words sprung from? She didn't really want to go to his home, did she? Her own ambivalence was unsettling. She didn't know herself anymore, and that was the scariest thing of all.

Sliding off the end of the bed, Jared came to stand in front of her.

"Why wait? Let's go now," he urged, his right hand capturing her chin to tilt her head up. Raising his left arm, he cast a quick glance at his watch. "It's not quite four now. If we get cracking, we could pack,

load the cars, eat an early supper, and be on the road
by six-thirty, seven at the latest. We could be home by
ten."

"But—"

Her attempt at protest was ended by the simple action of his parted lips meeting hers. There was no
passion in his kiss, no demand. With the contact of his
mouth he issued a silent, coaxing plea.

"Let's go home, boss lady," he verbalized the plea
when he lifted his head. "I have a yen to sleep in my
own bed tonight."

In her car, following Jared's showroom new, sporty-
looking Datsun through the early evening traffic, Nacia felt vaguely like she was hovering on hold in the eye
of a hurricane. The early squalls of the storm had
manifested themselves in the flurry of activity that had
followed her decision to go to his home.

Without her even hearing the sound of the whip
being snapped, she had been mobilized into action.
Clothes were thrown into suitcases, personal items
were tossed pell-mell into duffel and flight bags, and
all were loaded posthaste into their respective cars.

Before the reverberation of the slamming trunk
faded, Jared had dropped the room key at the motel
desk and was rushing her toward the nearest restaurant. There was no dawdling over after-supper coffee
this evening. There was no wine with dinner either; it
was strictly eat and move!

A grimace twisting her lips, Nacia braked a bare
three inches away from the gleaming black Datsun at
a long line waiting for a light to blink from red to
green. Some high-powered executive type you are, she

upbraided herself. You've been hustled like a wide-eyed innocent! Heck, Tracy would be harder to manipulate.

What really bothered her, though, was knowing that the strongest part of the storm awaited her at the end of the journey. The idea of indulging in a tell-all discussion with Jared made her very, very uncomfortable.

Nacia shifted in the bucket seat as she eased her foot off the brake, relieved at having to shelve her tormenting thoughts to concentrate on getting herself out of the city in one piece.

Once she was cruising along the Atlantic City Expressway at a steady fifty-five miles an hour it was a different story. There was nothing to do *but* think.

Although the cerebral exercise made her extremely uncomfortable, she forced herself to the task, hoping to make some sense of the relationship she'd entered into with Jared Ranklin.

How, she wondered, could she reconcile her behavior of the past week with the cold hostility she'd maintained toward men for the past fourteen years? Nacia shook her head in disbelief. Then, to compound her initial idiocy, she'd meekly agreed to spend a week alone with him in his home!

What the deuce had possessed her—besides him, that is? In less than ten hours of being introduced to her he had attacked her! And less than ten hours after that she had wantonly given herself to him. There definitely had to be a short in both her mental and physical circuits. Freud would have had a field day with her!

Nacia was almost grateful to the maniacal driver that tore around her as she neared the Walt Whitman Bridge, for he jolted her out of her introspection.

"Idiot doesn't believe there's a hell," she muttered, easing her foot off the gas pedal to accommodate her speed to the converging traffic.

From the bridge she followed the Datsun onto the Schuylkill Expressway where, at the Wissahickon exit, she was tempted to veer off and head for home. Cursing herself for a fool, she followed him anyway onto Route 202. She had passed several road signs advertising businesses in Norristown when the Datsun's turn signal began to blink and Jared pulled onto a secondary road. She was beginning to think he was going to drive right off the end of the earth, when his turn signal flashed on again and he made a sharp right between two brick entrance pillars. If possible, the private driveway was even darker than the road had been, and bumpy, too.

Her car's headlights illuminated dark tree trunks standing sentinel along the long drive. The two red taillights in front of her flickered and then the Datsun's headlights bathed a brick two-car garage in a golden glow. The glow became a glare as Nacia crawled to a stop alongside the Datsun.

There was the thunk of a car door closing, and a moment later Jared's long shadow darkened the white garage doors. As he cut through the glare, he held up his index finger in a wait-one-minute signal. His long stride carried him quickly to a door at the far end of the garage. He touched a button and immediately the surrounding area was washed in the blaze of a large dusk-to-dawn light positioned on the corner of the garage roof.

Nacia blinked against the assault on her eyes before releasing the door and stepping onto the rough macadam. It felt good to stand erect, and as she watched Jared walk to her she absentmindedly rubbed one palm over her derriere.

"Tired?" His low-pitched voice crooned sympathetically as he came to a stop close to her. One hand circled her waist and moved down, reflecting the soothing action of her massaging palm.

"Yes," Nacia responded on an indrawn breath. "And hungry. And thirsty." Her lips curved in a small smile. "And, if I don't find a bathroom soon, I'm afraid I'll explode."

His warm breath feathered her face with his softly expelled laughter. "We can't have that." His massaging hand returned to her waist. "Come along, lady love. I'll point you in the right direction, then come back for our gear."

Swinging around, he skirted the front of her car and led the way to a covered breezeway that connected the garage to the house.

Jared's hand touched a switch as he crossed the threshold, allowing Nacia to walk into a room that could have been featured in *House Beautiful*. She had little time to admire the room's appointments, however, as Jared motioned her to follow him across the flagstone-patterned tile to a pair of louvered swinging doors opening onto a hallway that obviously led to the front door.

As she stepped past the louvered panel he held open for her, he indicated a door to the left. "Right in there," he told her.

Nacia walked out of the powder room just as Jared shoved his way through the swinging door, a suitcase in each hand, the short straps of his duffel bag over one shoulder, the long strap of her flight bag over the other.

"Here, let me take something!" she offered, reaching for the case in his left hand.

"Not necessary." Jared shook his head, then tilted it forward. "If you'll precede me and hit the light switches, I'll lug this stuff."

Shrugging lightly, Nacia moved out ahead of him down the shadowy hall.

"To the right of the front door you'll find three switches; flip the first two," he directed quietly.

Following his instructions, Nacia turned on the lights. The first thing that registered was that she was standing on the second level of a trilevel structure. To her right, a delicate-looking wrought-iron barrier ran out about four feet, ending at five steps that descended into a large square living room. On her left, two doors were set into the wall that ran from the front of the house to the kitchen, the first approximately three feet from where she stood, the second twelve or thirteen feet away. Five feet directly in front of her, Jared stood, patiently waiting at the foot of a short flight of stairs. The powder room she had moments ago vacated was set into and under that staircase.

"At the risk of sounding like a nag," he drawled, "I'd appreciate it if you'd contain your curiosity about the house till after I've divested myself of these bags."

His head moved to indicate the stairway. "At the top of these stairs you'll find two doors. The one to the right is my bathroom, the other my bedroom, inside of which is yet another light switch." He smiled dryly. "If you will?"

As she mounted the six stairs, Nacia asked herself what she thought she was doing. Here she was, leading the way to a bedroom in another woman's house. The fact that the other woman was now dead was immaterial; her touch had to be everywhere—most especially in the bedroom she now hesitated in front of.

"Na-cia!" Jared's exasperation was evidenced by the way he drew her name out. With the verbal nudge her hand grasped the knob. As the door swung in, she groped for the wall switch.

The room that sprang into relief was very large, sparsely furnished, and totally devoid of any feminine touches.

Even so, Nacia suddenly knew she did not want to spend the night in the oversize bed that was taking up so much of the floor space.

With a relieved sigh, Jared dropped the cases on the gleaming hardwood floor at the foot of the bed. Flexing his shoulders, he turned, a frown creasing his brow at the sight of her stiffened form and withdrawn expression.

"You don't like the room?" His meaning had little to do with the room, and Nacia knew it.

"Yes, of course I like it, but—" Nacia paused to wet her lips.

"There's always a but," Jared mimicked her own taunt of nearly a week ago. "Let's hear it, boss lady."

The only way to get to the point was to get to the point. "Jared, I think I'd better go home."

His gaze sliced to his watch, then back to her face. "Are you nuts!" he exclaimed, if softly. "It's ten of ten. You're not going anywhere at this time of night. Not alone, anyway."

Nacia bristled at his tone, even though it didn't surprise her. She'd been wondering when the supreme male would resurface.

"I'll go where I want, *when* I want," she said clearly. "With or without your permission. Coming here was a mistake. I don't belong here—with a man I know nothing about, in another woman's home."

Crossing the space that separated them in three long strides, Jared, his features set in grim determination, grasped her upper arms tightly.

"This is not, and never has been, another woman's home," he grated harshly. "My wife didn't live to see its completion." He drew a deep breath in an obvious attempt at control. "I decide who does and does not belong here, and—"

"Jared," Nacia inserted warningly, "you're hurting me."

He loosened his hold before going on. "And if you know nothing about me, it's only because you chose not to know." A spasm of an unidentifiable emotion rippled over his face. "Correct me if I'm wrong," he went on, somewhat sarcastically, "but weren't we going to spend this coming week learning about each other?"

"Yes," Nacia admitted, then hedged, "but I—"

"Damn the buts," Jared cut her off roughly. "What's really squirming around in your head, Nacia?'' Before she could even open her mouth he answered for her. ''It's this room. *My* room. Sharing a bed in an impersonal motel room is one thing. Sharing *my* bed, in *my* room, is something altogether different, isn't it?'' Again he would allow her no time to respond. ''It's easy to escape into fantasy in a motel room in a resort town, but reality has a way of intruding into a private room in a private home, right?''

That he'd read her emotional conflict so easily made her nervous. It also made her angry. If he thought for one second she'd admit that his shot had struck the target, she fumed, he could just think again!

''Out of my way, Jared,'' she ordered coldly.

''No.'' His tone held flat finality.

''You can't keep me here against my will,'' she pointed out reasonably.

''Can't I?'' he gibed.

Something about his eyes, the slight curve at the corners of his mouth, sent a thrill—of what? Apprehension? Anticipation?—down her spine.

''Of course you can't.'' Who, she wondered, was she trying to convince—him or herself? ''How could you?''

''By taking your clothes away from you?'' he inquired blandly.

''You wouldn't!'' She doubted that he'd go to such lengths to keep her there. ''Would you?''

''No, I wouldn't.'' The curve at his lips changed to a definite twitch. ''On the other hand,'' he mused aloud, the twitch growing, ''I might consider sabotaging your car.''

''Jared Ranklin, don't you dare touch my car!''

"Okay, I won't," he agreed, laughing. "On one condition," he qualified.

Nacia knew, but she asked anyway. "And that is?"

His smile told her he knew she knew. "You stay with me through the week. Coming here *was* your choice, you know," he reminded her softly. "You don't have to sleep in this room. You can stay in the guest room."

"Alone?" Willing herself not to be affected by his fingers that were now tormenting the soft skin of her upper arm, Nacia eyed him warily.

"If you insist," Jared conceded with obvious reluctance.

Nacia bit her lip to suppress a shiver of response to his now wandering hands. "You promise you won't force the issue?"

The change in him was immediate and chilling. His body grew rigid with anger, and he dropped his hands to his sides and stepped back. "You're not ever going to let me forget that first night, are you?" His voice had a strained, strangled sound, as if forced through teeth clenched against pain.

"Jared, I didn't—"

"Every time you think you need a lever," he gritted accusingly, "or a weapon, you'll trot that out and rap me with it. Won't you?"

Appalled as much by his look as his accusation, she stepped close to place a placating hand on his taut forearm. His narrowing eyes shifted to her hand, and then he deliberately moved his arm from under the touch. His action hurt, almost as much as his bitter words had.

"Jared, please, I wasn't referring to that night. I wasn't even thinking of it." For some obscure reason she couldn't begin to decipher, Nacia felt she had to make him believe her. His skeptical expression revealed she had not quite succeeded. "I'm in no position to throw stones, as far as that night is concerned."

This seemed to confuse him, for he frowned. "What do you mean?" he demanded a little uncertainly.

Nacia sighed, suddenly tired of it all. "It doesn't matter now." She ventured a conciliatory smile. "Does the offer of a room include board as well? We had an early supper, which you rushed me through, and I'm starving."

The easing of tension in him was a visible thing, beginning with the softening of his eyes. Catching her hand in his, he rubbed his thumb over the back of it from her wrist to the tip of her fingers. "You'll stay?" he asked quietly.

"Yes."

"The entire week?" he pushed.

Nacia intended to say no, or maybe, or we'll see, but she couldn't stop herself. "Yes." So much for firm intentions, she mused wryly.

He stood still for a moment, simply staring into her eyes; then he leaned forward to brush warm lips over her cheek. "No force, lady love," he promised. "No pressure. We'll play it by ear, do what comes naturally. Okay?"

"If I don't fade away from lack of nourishment," she chided in a bid to dispel the sensuality that was beginning to shimmer between them.

His other hand lifted to her waist, then drifted testingly down over her rounded hip. "I don't think there's much chance of your fading away,'' he teased. Then he lifted his hand and gave her a light smack. ''But, come on, we'll go see what we can go scrounge up in the kitchen.''

Turning away, Jared bent to pick up her case and flight bag, straightening with a start when she delivered a resounding blow to his prominent posterior with her palm.

''What the hell—?'' he yelped, swinging around to glare at her.

''If you kiss me, do you expect me to kiss you back?'' Nacia asked sweetly, innocently.

''Yes, but—''

''Expect me always to respond in kind,'' she warned, all traces of sweetness gone.

''Nacia, I did not hurt you with that love pat,'' he sighed. ''It didn't mean anything—''

''I know,'' she interrupted impatiently. ''That's the sad, frustrating thing. I truly doubt the majority of men *mean* anything by those little indignities they perpetrate on women. It's so ingrained that it's become an almost natural mode of behavior. In fact, I'd be willing to bet few men ever pause to think of the insult they're offering every time they deliver one of their actions that doesn't *mean* anything.''

Fully expecting his ridicule, Nacia stood straight, waiting for something that didn't come. Instead, he remained still, a considering frown drawing his brows together. When, finally, he did express his opinion, he surprised her completely by concurring with her.

''You're right, you know. I've never thought about it.'' His grin was boyish, and utterly disarming. ''But in my own defense I must protest that I do not make a habit of patting females on the rump." His grin became downright devilish. "Only the ones I'm attempting to lure into my bed."

Nacia was exasperated but she couldn't keep from laughing. Snatching up the flight bag, she spun away from him.

"Oh, let's go find something to eat."

Amusement quirking his lips, Jared followed her down the short flight of stairs, calling her to a halt at the door nearest the kitchen.

"The guest room," he intoned, sober-faced, swinging the door open with a flourish.

The room was just that—a place for the infrequent overnight guest to sleep. The furniture was an unprepossessing matched set in maple. The drapes, bedspread and carpeting were all in the same sandy beige. The decorations consisted of two lamps, both with cream-colored shades, and an ashtray.

After slinging her case onto the single bed, Jared pointed at a door on the near wall. "The bathroom is through there. It connects to my daughter's bedroom at the front of the house." His eyes swept the room dismissingly. "I hope you'll be uncomfortable here."

"Jared."

"Well." His shrug was eloquent. "If you *are* uncomfortable, maybe you'll join me upstairs."

Unable to dredge up a retort cutting enough, Nacia sailed by him and out the door, heading for sustenance. She had a feeling she was going to need all the fortification she could get.

Inside the swinging doors she paused to take stock of the kitchen, ignoring Jared as he passed her on his way to take stock of the refrigerator.

No wife would have cause to complain of a lack of storage space in here, Nacia mused, her gaze examining the dark wood cabinets on three of the walls. The area around the wall and base cabinets was covered by rusty red brick. The appliances were all in a copper tone. The remaining wall around a large window was papered with a mustard-colored burlap weave. In front of the windows was a rectangular butcher-block-topped table. Neatly in place around the table were four captain's chairs.

Nacia was examining the philodendron planted in a copper teapot and placed on a lacy place mat in the center of the table when Jared's voice drew her away from the consideration of whether or not the healthy-looking plant needed water.

"I'm afraid the selection is limited," he drawled from around the refrigerator door. "The milk's sour, I wouldn't want to trust the lunch meat, and even if I did, it wouldn't be of much use because the bread is dead." Allowing the door to swing shut, he opened the smaller freezer door. After a quick perusal of the freezer's contents, he glanced at her. "How does pizza grab you?"

"Fine." Nacia crossed the room to him. "Anything, as long as it's filling. Can I help?"

"Yeah, you can get the table ready while I toss this into the microwave. You'll find a dishcloth in the top drawer in the cabinet next to the sink," he directed, placing frozen rectangular pieces of pizza on a glass tray he'd withdrawn from a wall cabinet. "The plates are to the right in the cabinet above the sink, the glasses to the left."

They worked in silence a few moments. Nacia wiped the table, then set the luncheon plates on it, while Jared put the pizza in the microwave. The timer pinged just as she opened the cabinet door to her left.

"Do you want water, Jared?"

"Water?" Jared gave her a pained expression before swinging open the refrigerator door once more. "Take out the stemmed glasses," he ordered, turning away from the fridge to flourish a bottle of white wine.

The pizza was so hot it singed her tongue. The wine was so cold it chilled her teeth.

"Do you always keep your wine in the refrigerator?" she gasped.

"Yes," he answered blandly. "I don't like my wine chilled. I like it cold."

"Obviously." Nacia took another, smaller sip from the delicate fluted glass. "A wine connoisseur would probably frown on the practice," she observed.

"Probably," Jared agreed dryly. "But, then, I couldn't care less what a wine connoisseur—or a connoisseur of any kind, for that matter—frowns on. I'm my own connoisseur." He lifted his glass in a mocking salute. "*Laissez-faire,* sweetheart."

"Really? Live and let live, and all that?" she taunted.

"Right on target," he concurred emphatically.

Nacia thought about this as she chewed on her last bit of pizza. "Mmm," she murmured, wiping her lips free of crumbs with a paper napkin. "Yet you were prepared to tamper with my car to keep me here."

"No!" Jared denied roughly, tossing his own napkin onto his plate. "I was just making a noise. I wouldn't have touched your car. I didn't like the idea of you driving alone so late at night, and—'' he shrugged ''—I wanted you to stay.'' He finished his wine with a few deep swallows. His eyes seemed to fasten on her lips as Nacia, suddenly parched, emptied her glass.

Rising with slow deliberation, he came to her, grasping her arms to draw her to her feet before him. Bending to her, he brushed his lips over her cheek.

''That's not exactly true,'' he qualified his last statement. ''What I really want,'' he sighed, ''is to be back in the motel, in bed, in you.'' His lips teased the outer edge of her ear, his tongue darting into the recess when she shivered in response. ''I would have thought that by now this urgency I feel to have you would have been satisfied,'' he murmured raggedly. ''But it is every bit as strong as that first night.'' His fingers tightened spasmodically on her arms. ''There is one difference.'' Jared's tone firmed. ''There's the door; you may walk out of here whenever you wish.'' His hands loosened, then began moving caressingly down her back. His teeth gently nipped at her lobe. ''I want you now every bit as badly as I wanted you that first night, but I won't apply any pressure this time.''

Desire unwinding insidiously inside her, her breathing constricted, Nacia's voice had a strangled, desperate sound.

''Wh-what do you call what you're doing now?''

He laughed softly, and his warm breath teased her skin tantalizingly.

''Seducing you, I hope.'' The amusement in his tone was replaced with deadly earnestness. ''I want to hear you say you'll stay the week as agreed.''

"I'll stay the week as agreed," Nacia repeated. All of her reasons for denying him had become a confused jumble in her mind. Jared exhaled slowly, deeply, revealing to her that he'd been holding his breath.

"Come to bed, love."

For long intense seconds, Jared stood perfectly still, savoring the mixture of release and excitement that vied for supremacy as they raced through his tense body.

You've been given yet another chance, he chastened himself sternly. Do not, repeat, do not blow it this time. This woman is a stranger to gentleness from the opposite sex. For some reason she is not yet ready to talk about, she expects you to use force, either physical or emotional. With your own actions and stupidity you have damn well confirmed her fears. Now, stop thinking with your senses and use your head, or chances are you are going to lose her.

This last consideration sent a streak of alarm coursing through him. She was the sum total of everything he had worked for, existed for, his whole life. If by his own carelessness he let her slip away from him, he would deserve all the pain and anguish he would doubtlessly have to endure.

Do not assume the role of conqueror, he told himself. In the end, this woman will not be conquered. Your first victory over her body does not count. If she closes her mind to you you're a goner. Put a leash on your needs and desires and grip it tightly. Give her all the room and breathing space she requires. Move slowly, speak gently, proceed with caution; the emotional life you save may be your own.

It was at that moment that Jared recognized the bounds of love constricting his actions. He was not surprised by the depth of his feelings for Nacia. Hadn't he been halfway in love with the illusion of her before he'd ever laid eyes on her? He had known it long before the sight of her crossing the beach to join Frank had made him catch his breath. He was in love with her.

Chapter 7

Nacia was not swept off her feet, into his arms, and carried up the staircase in the grand romantic fashion.

In fact, with her murmured acquiescence, Jared released her and took one step back. His eyes, smokily dark from the fire burning within, held hers with relentless intensity. Moving slowly, as if not wanting to startle her, he lifted his hand, palm up in silent invitation.

The action itself was a seducement. Nacia succumbed without a murmur, unhesitatingly covering his palm with her own. In a silence that was quivering with passion, she preceded him out of the kitchen, along the hall, and up the short flight of stairs, not once giving consideration to her previous intention of sleeping in the guest room.

Strangely, the closing of his bedroom door behind them instilled in Nacia an unfamiliar, oddly reassuring sensation of being safe and protected, almost as if they were locked inside a world of their very own, separate and apart from life's hurtful and mundane realities.

On one level of her consciousness, Nacia knew that Jared's silently extended hand, the way he had moved to the side, allowing her to lead the way to his bedroom, were all calculated to reassure her regarding his promise of no pressure.

Still without speaking, Jared walked to her. Raising his hands, he slowly, carefully, began undressing her, the gentle touch of his trembling fingers approaching reverence.

"I don't understand it . . . this . . . whatever it is between us." His deep voice quavered, sending shards of anticipation through Nacia. "I'm not going to question it either. Not tonight, anyway."

Divested of the protective barrier of clothes, Nacia stood before him proudly. The shiver that rippled over her skin was not caused by the air-conditioning.

The tips of his fingers investigated the curves of her neck, her shoulders, her collarbone before drifting down to the aching mounds of her breasts.

"What I do understand is that with no other woman, not even my wife, have I ever experienced this—" he hesitated, as if grasping for the right word "—this overriding need."

Still he only touched her with the tips of his fingers. The light touch of the hardening tips of her breasts drew an electrified gasp from her parted lips. He moved on to her waist, then outlined the mature flare of her hips. Where hipline blended into thigh, the trailing fingers changed direction to trek on an angle up and over the gentle mound of her abdomen. When they met, one palm was laid lightly but possessively against her warm skin.

Nacia was beyond questioning why his feathery exploration of her should have such a shattering effect. She was beyond questioning anything. All conscious thought had given way to the senses. She saw the odd combination of strain and tenderness on his face. She heard the erratic unevenness of his breathing. She smelled the enticement of his perspiration-sheened skin. All her senses conspiring against her, Nacia felt his light fingertip touch in the deepest recess of her being. If his breathing was uneven, hers was practically nonexistent.

One by one life's acquired layers had dropped away. Gone was the facade of the coolheaded business executive. Gone was the shell of disdain for the male of the species. Gone was the lovingly concerned parent. What remained, glorying in his sight, quivering at his touch, was a basic, unadorned woman yearning for her man.

Jared was evidently experiencing something similar, because he, too, was having trouble articulating his thoughts. "I know I should feel shame for my behavior that first night. I know I *should* but I can't, and I don't." He wet his lips, as if making the admission had robbed his mouth of all moisture. "It's hard for a man—at least this man—to admit to a total loss of control, but I do admit to it. I broke under the pressure of a need the likes of which I'd never known."

Under the circumstances, Nacia barely heard Jared's words. It would be a long time before they coalesced in her mind, making her aware that he'd bared his soul to her. For now, it was the low tremor of his voice, not the content of his words, that she heard.

"I do regret frightening you, hurting you, but—" He broke off, the palm of his hand moving in an erotic pattern until it covered her breast. "But I can't feel shame for what was the beginning of the most satisfying experience I've ever known." Again his hand moved, this time to gently cup her face.

"Nacia, Nacia," he murmured her name in a prayerlike whisper. "You've given me your body so beautifully over the last week. Let me have this next week to try to earn your trust."

At that point Nacia would have allowed him any wish if it would have hastened his descending mouth. In her bemused fascination with his lips, drawing with excruciating slowness to her own, she willingly granted him the week, never realizing she was bestowing much, much more.

"If that's what you want," she whispered.

"It is," Jared groaned, "starting tomorrow. Tonight I want to make love to you until all thought of anyone or anything else is wiped from your mind, and all you know is me and the pleasure we give each other."

Finally the distance was closed. Mouth touched mouth in what was more than a kiss. Through the medium of his lips Jared bestowed a benediction, a seal, and, though Nacia did not then recognize it, a commitment.

What Nacia did recognize was the melting warmth, the cramping ache pervading the core of her femininity. It lent strength to her arms as they circled his neck, and weakened her legs so that she sagged against him.

Feeling her weakness, Jared wrapped his arms around her, drawing her close to his own hard strength. His kiss changed, departing the sphere of the near spiritual to enter the realm of the purely sensual. His tongue dipped delicately into the moist recess of her mouth, tasting, testing, stroking gently until she thought she'd go mad with his teasing.

Soft, whimpering moans vibrated in her throat, and she undulated sensuously against him as she dug her fingers into his crisp, dark curls to press his head closer, fusing their lips together.

Jared's response was swift and aggressive. His tongue stiffened and plunged, again and again. His arms tightened convulsively, crushing the breath out of her, infusing fire into her. She felt herself being moved, then lowered to the mattress. All the while his stroking tongue evoked anticipation of a fuller possession. When he pulled away from her, Nacia gave a soft, incoherent cry of protest.

"I'll be right back, love," he soothed, dipping his head to kiss her quickly, gently. "I must get out of my clothes. I want to feel every inch of you against me."

His shoes and socks were the first to go; then, standing, he unashamedly removed his short-sleeved pullover before releasing the snap and zipper on his jeans and sliding them, along with his briefs, over his hips and down his long legs. It was only after the clothes lay littering the floor that he turned away, one hand searching in the narrow drawer in the night-stand by the bed.

Watching his slightly bent figure, a tiny, gentle smile played around the corners of her mouth. Jared had been scrupulous in keeping his promise of protection of her. When he turned back to her she held her arms out to him in welcome.

Jared took one step then stopped, his eyes sweeping the length of her from her wildly tangled hair to her slim ankles at the end of her long, slender legs. "You look so beautifully wanton," he whispered when, at last, she felt the brush of his chest against her breasts. "I hate to think of any other man ever seeing you like this."

"No other man ever has," she told him truthfully, unaware of exactly how very much she was revealing to him.

Jared was not quick to claim her. Slowly, expertly, using his hands and fingers, his lips and tongue, he found and paid homage to her most sensitive spots. By the time his hard thighs nudged against the inner softness of hers she was a fiery torch, burning only for him.

Flame met flame, and for sweet, tormenting moments the blaze consumed them. A half breath after she cried his name aloud, his own hoarse cry echoed hers. In the ember of the dying flame, he stroked her, caressed her, praised her until her eyelids lowered in concession to exhaustion.

A numbness in her side woke Nacia from the contented near-sleep. Jared's fragrant, wine-scented breath warmed her skin on the side of her neck; his replete, relaxed body covered half of hers, one leg resting in the cradle of her thighs.

As she came to full consciousness, Nacia's mind filled with the wonder of the experience she had shared with him mere moments—or was it hours?—ago. He had been gentle and rough, demanding and pleading, the conqueror and the conquered. In the deepest recess of her mind Nacia knew, but was not yet ready to face, that he had been all things male to all things female in her.

Her mind busy shying away from the hows and whys of it all, she absently stroked the nape of his neck. Raising her hand a fraction, she trailed her smooth oval nails along the curve of his spine. The length of her arm allowed her to go no farther than the middle of his back where, after hesitating an instant, she drew four lines to the point of his shoulder. The first indication that he was not asleep came in the form of a rippling shudder, and a gasp.

"Oh, God, Nacia, it's happening all over again," he groaned. He stirred, burying his face into her neck.

"Ouch, Jared, your hipbone is digging into me!"

"Darling, I'm sorry!" Using his forearm, Jared levered his body up and over her own. His legs came together between her thighs. "Better?" he crooned, his soothing hand rubbing the circulation back to her numb limb.

"Yes."

"You know what you've done now, don't you?"

"Jared, I'm half-asleep." Though she was tired, she smiled beguilingly. Never having participated in teasing love games, Nacia was surprised at how easily she learned the moves.

Jared's eyes gleamed in appreciation of her first foray into the field. "Then I'll just have to wake you up," he threatened, his smile rakish. "Part by part and piece by piece."

They teased and tormented each other, laughing in delight, gasping with pleasure until, each in a frenzy for the other, they came together wildly, their laughter replaced by deep-throated sounds of lovemaking.

"What went wrong with your marriage?"

Nacia had spent the morning wondering when the first question would come; even so, she was unprepared for Jared's bluntness.

Her serenely composed features revealing none of the conflicting emotions churning inside, Nacia picked up her coffee cup. Playing for time, she sipped tentatively at the steaming brew.

Surprisingly, considering their exhausted state when they'd finally drifted off to sleep, they had wakened early, within minutes of each other. After sharing a shower—a conservation precaution, Jared assured her dryly, as it had been extremely dry for several weeks—they both dressed in jeans and cotton shirts, then went directly to Jared's car to go shopping for much-needed groceries.

On returning from the supermarket, Jared had put the groceries away while Nacia cooked breakfast.

Now, the remnants of their meal cluttering the table, she knew her period of grace was over.

"Don't you remember?" Jared prodded. "Or is this silence your way of telling me to mind my own business?" His teasing tone didn't quite succeed in masking his impatience.

"No," Nacia denied, her head moving slowly from side to side. "But it happened so long ago. Is it really important now?"

"Yes, I think it is." Jared's gaze captured hers. "I think your attitude today can be related to the failure of your marriage."

"Attitude?" Nacia frowned. "What attitude?"

Jared smiled—almost. "Your attitude to men, mainly."

"To men?" Nacia frowned again. Jared's expression left her in little doubt that he was unimpressed with her pretense at confusion.

"To men," he echoed mockingly. "That superior, condescending, contemptuous attitude of yours."

Recoiling in shock, Nacia stared at him in utter disbelief. Was this the same man who had made love to her with a gentleness reminiscent of near adoration? Could this be the same man who had whispered words of beguiling sweetness to her? The contrast between the man between the sheets and the man facing her across the breakfast table was like black and white. Or, Nacia concluded sadly, day and night.

Her emotions churning with a mixture of anger and pain from his unexpected verbal thrust, she didn't pause to question why Jared's words could inflict wounds that caused more pain than anything Clay had ever said to her.

Moving stiffly, Nacia pushed back her chair and stood up, conscious of Jared's steady regard. His quiet voice arrested her as she moved to walk away.

"What's the matter, lover, did I hit a nerve?"

"Don't call me that!" Nacia exclaimed sharply.

"Why not?" Jared's smile held more pity than amusement. "We *are* lovers."

An irrefutable fact. A fact, moreover, that Nacia was having considerable difficulty dealing with. Why didn't she just walk away from him? she asked herself bleakly. All the way away from him. Out of his kitchen, out of his house, out of his life. Hard on the heels of that thought came a sharp memory of his mouth crushing hers, his hands inflicting sweet torture, his hard body possessing while being possessed. Senses warring with common sense held her in indecision.

"We'll never get anywhere this way," he sighed. "Sit down, Nacia, please."

Reinforced by his coaxing tone, her senses won the brief war. Her spine still stiff, Nacia sank back down onto her chair. Perched on the end of her chair, she watched as he reached for the coffeepot, refilling her cup without bothering to inquire if she wanted it.

"Okay, let's start again," he said quietly after topping off his own coffee. "What went wrong with your marriage?"

"Everything." Nacia's tone was as stiff as her spine.

"What everything?" Jared persisted.

"Everything everything," she retorted, goaded into sarcasm. "He didn't like my cooking. He didn't like the way I kept the apartment. He didn't like the way I dressed. He didn't like my job." Nacia shrugged dismissively. "As I said—everything."

A frown pulled Jared's brows together. "He had to like something, he married you. Or were you—"

"No." Nacia answered the question before he'd finished asking it. "But he didn't object when I became pregnant within the first year." Nacia's smile was bitter with memory. "Like most men, Clay considered the topic of birth control a bore."

"Not most men," Jared objected strongly. When Nacia gave him a sardonic look, he qualified his flat statement. "At least, not anymore. Today most men are as concerned about birth control as women are."

"Except when they lose control, or get carried away in the heat of the moment." Nacia tossed the barb at him in a deceptively cool voice. An oddly sick feeling invaded her stomach at the pained expression that fleetingly shadowed his face.

"You use words like a weapon," he muttered harshly. "Can I look forward to a hatchet job every time I correctly counter one of your sweeping condemnations?"

"Jared..." Nacia's voice trailed off; there was really no way to defend herself. She had been verbally slapping men down for so long that it had become automatic.

His frustration evidenced by a hissing sigh, Jared got to his feet and began clearing the table. "We got sidetracked again, didn't we?" He was standing beside her, a plate in each hand.

Nodding in answer, she got up to help him. They worked in a strained silence until the kitchen was once again tidy, avoiding any physical contact as they went about their individual tasks. After folding the dishcloth, Nacia turned from the sink to find herself face-to-face with a sober-looking Jared.

"Do we continue?" he asked in a tone devoid of expression.

"I...suppose so."

Her hesitation, as brief as it was, produced an explosion.

"Dammit, Nacia, what is it with you, anyway?" His eyes seemed to shoot blue sparks at her. "Does talking about him still hurt? Do you still love him?"

"Love him!" she cried. "I hate him."

The fire in his eyes was concealed by narrowing lids. "And all other men in the bargain, right?"

Nacia glared at him, determined to stare him down. She couldn't; Jared returned her stare with cold intent.

"Right," she snapped.

With sudden swiftness he grasped her wrist and strode to the swinging doors, dragging her behind him.

Certain he was going to use the typical method of subduing dissension with bedroom athletics, Nacia jerked her arm in a futile attempt to dislodge his steel-like clasp on her wrist. "Jared, stop this!"

At that moment Jared was not a very attractive sight. His features were set in grim determination; his mouth was a thin, slashing line in his face. Storming through the doors and along the hall, he surprised her by circling around the stairs and stomping down the five steps to the living room where, with a seemingly effortless flick of his arm, he directed her toward the long velvet-covered sofa.

Furious at being manhandled, Nacia immediately jumped to her feet. "How dare you try and—"

"Stay put," Jared ordered, quietly but firmly pushing her back onto the cushion. "Okay," he went on with chilling calmness, "I assume I'm included in that blanket condemnation. In fact, by now I've probably taken over the number one spot on the list.

But that's okay too, when you're at the top, there's nowhere to go but down." He stood before her, hands on his slim hips, looking very tall, and very intimidating. "It explains a lot. The way you talk to men, the way you *look* at men—as if they were beneath your notice."

His hard-eyed stare bored into her. "I find it impossible to believe that you learned to hate the entire male population simply because you could not please one member of it. There's more to it than that." Jared drew a deep breath, then released it slowly. "I want to hear about it, all about it, and you're not getting off that sofa until I do."

Trembling with anger, Nacia glared at him impotently. He could back up his assertion and she knew it. His settled-in stance and the resolute set of his face left no doubt whatever that if he wanted her confined to the sofa for a week, a week was exactly how long she'd be there.

Damn him! Nacia raged silently. She didn't want to talk about Clay. She didn't even want to think about him!

"I'm waiting."

Nacia bristled. "You have no right to pry into my per—"

"Oh, knock it off," he interrupted impatiently. "For God's sake, Nacia, we've been sleeping together for a week now, and I—"

"And you think that gives you the right to crawl inside my mind?" Nacia's bitter question cut across his tense voice.

"Right or not, that's precisely what I'm going to do. Willing or not, *boss* lady, I'm going to pump you dry.

So get on with it.'' He shrugged carelessly. ''What's the big deal, anyway?''

''Subjugation.'' Nacia spat the word at him. ''Degradation. Humiliation. *That's* the big deal. It sickens me to remember it, let alone talk about it.'' Lifting her chin, she faced the now rigid form of her inquisitor.

''It's very hard to imagine any one man having that kind of power over you,'' Jared opined in an oddly tight tone.

''I was not thirty-five then, Jared,'' she snapped. ''I was twenty years old and—'' a bitter smile twisted her lips ''—I thought I was in love.'' Her laughter was short-lived, and not very pleasant to hear. ''Love! How quaint. The fruits of my love were bruises on the outside, scars on the inside, and a child he denied.''

One word appeared to electrify him. ''Bruises,'' he repeated grimly. ''He physically abused you?''

''Yes.''

Closing his eyes briefly, Jared exhaled slowly. ''And I came on like a one-man army.'' His hands dropped limply to his side, fingers flexing. ''Oh, hell, honey,'' he groaned, ''you have every reason to hate me.''

All the anger and tension drained out of Nacia. What right did she have to be so angry? She had known Jared was full of questions about her when she'd agreed to come to his house; he had been perfectly frank about his curiosity.

A twinge of pain drew her gaze to her lap and her tightly clasped hands lying there. She was behaving foolishly, she knew it, yet it had been so very long since she'd confided in anyone. Both her mother and her sister Jean had long ago given up trying to get her to discuss anything personal. Sighing deeply, she consciously loosened her fingers.

"I don't hate you, Jared," she murmured, raising her eyes to his. Something suspiciously like a shudder traveled the length of his body, and his taut features relaxed into a relieved smile.

"May I get up now?"

At her meek tone, his smile stretched into a grin. Stepping back, he executed a sweeping bow. "You have the run of the house, my lady," he invited teasingly, then cautioned, "just don't run too far."

"Your magnanimity underwhelms me," Nacia teased back, taking swift advantage of his offer by rising and walking to the large square window set into the side wall.

Strolling across the highly glossed hardwood floor, Nacia let her gaze roam around the large square room. There were two squat, deeply padded chairs in the same silvery blue velvet that covered the long sofa, and an invitingly comfortable-looking recliner in a contrasting heather tweed. Two square and one octagonal table in pecan wood were placed conveniently close to the chairs, the rich patina of the wood gleaming in the bright morning sunlight. Shiny brass-based lamps and several strategically placed porcelain pieces betrayed a female touch.

A natural stone fireplace took up most of the far wall. An archway in the remaining wall led into a large dining room.

"I like this room," Nacia noted, glancing back at Jared as she came to a stop at the window.

Jared's grin settled back into a soft smile. "I'm glad." His gaze followed the path hers had taken. "Joyce decorated it."

The name rang a memory bell. "Your daughter?"

"Yes."

Nacia's glance skimmed the room again. "How old is she?"

"She'll be seventeen in September." Jared's voice was rich with parental pride. "She'll be entering college next fall. She's going to study interior design." As he was speaking he walked to her. "How old is your daughter, Nacia?"

"Fourteen." This time there was no hesitation in her answer. "And at this point in her life, I think she's studying boys."

"And you don't object to that?"

Nacia frowned. "No. The obsession with boys is normal in fourteen-year-old girls, isn't it?"

"Yes, of course." Jared nodded emphatically. "But considering your own attitude toward the male sex, I couldn't help but wonder if you would object."

Nacia was caught in her own trap. "I'm afraid I overstated the emotional case." A wry smile touched her lips. "I don't hate the entire male sex, just one member of it."

"But you don't *like* us very much, do you?" Jared insisted. "Or aren't you even aware that you talk down to every man you come in contact with?"

Did she? Nacia considered his charge a moment. Yes, perhaps she did, but it was an unconscious condescension. Didn't most men deserve female scorn? Most men? The thought shook her with its implications. Unwilling to face the reason for her ambiguousness, Nacia swung around to stare out of the window.

"By and large, men have earned women's disdain." Though her tone was mild, it was firm with conviction. "The male has been riding roughshod over the female forever. His long day of supremacy is over. She has issued an intellectual challenge. Someday he will admit to her equality. Understandably, she grows impatient with his procrastination." She used the abstract in explanation of her own attitude. Lifting her sun-kissed auburn head, she slanted him a teasing glance. "There *are* some men who have conceded the right."

Jared's eyes gleamed in appreciation of her admission. "I hope you believe that I am one of those men."

"Is what I think so very important?" Nacia was sorry for the question the moment it was asked. It had too much the sound of a flirtatious probe. What was she playing at? she wondered vaguely. She had not sought a man's opinion of her since high school and her marriage to Clay.

"Yes, what you think is important." Nacia hadn't heard him move, but he was right behind her, his warm breath feathering her hair. "I was fully aware of your impression of me from the beginning. In your book I was a number one chauvinist jerk, right?"

Nacia whipped around, her protest drying on her lips at the realization of how very close to her he was.

Closing the mere inches between them, Jared brushed his mouth lightly over hers. "Don't feel you have to defend that opinion, it was the correct one." At her startled expression he smiled ruefully. "I *knew* I was coming on too strong from the first minute. But

I had anticipated our first meeting for so long, I'm ashamed to admit I overreacted."

Good going, blabbermouth, Jared scorned himself for the blurted admission. So far this morning you have managed to lose your patience, your temper, and now your protective cover. Keep up the good work and you just might manage to lose her, as well!

Jared had not planned on revealing quite so much, quite so soon. With a fatalistic mental shrug, he stoically prepared himself for the questions he could actually see forming in Nacia's auburn-topped head.

Oh, well, it had to come sooner or later. So thinking, he watched her, a gentle smile tugging at his lips. Nacia's eyes telegraphed her first query. Jared knew what she would say before she opened her mouth.

Chapter 8

Anticipated our first meeting! Nacia stared at Jared in bewilderment. What was he talking about?

"Jared, I don't understand," she said with forced steadiness. "How could you have anticipated our first meeting on the beach?"

"I didn't know it would be on the beach," he corrected gently, then grinned. "I didn't *know* it would be anywhere, as far as that goes." His shoulders moved in a light shrug. "I had hoped to meet you someday, somewhere."

"But—"

Jared slid his index finger over her lips to silence her. "No mystery, honey." The texture of her mouth seemed to fascinate him, for his eyes darkened as he observed the movement of his finger tracing the well-defined outline. "Frank had told me about you, and I wanted . . . hoped to meet you. Simple as that."

Eyes wide with shock, Nacia pulled back, away from his enticing fingertip touch. "Frank told you about me?" At his calm nod, she nearly shouted, "Told you what?"

"Not very much," Jared laughed softly. "Just enough to rouse my interest."

"How dare he!" she breathed, growing angrier by the minute. "How dare he discuss me with anyone, let alone other men!" Feeling the need to pace, Nacia attempted to move by him.

"Will you calm down? He actually said very little. Listen to me, you hothead!" His near shout brought her to instant stillness. "The only remarks he ever made were complimentary. Frank admires you very much. He seems to think that Uniforms Inc. would collapse if you ever decided to quit. He claims you are the strongest woman he has ever met." A devilish, knowing smile turned his lips up at the corners. "He's also of the opinion that you are sexy as hell. I think it was after he said that that I decided I had to meet you." The devil in him leered at her out of his dark eyes. "Perhaps," he murmured, "that was when I decided to have you."

A disquieting, cold sensation slithered through Nacia's insides. Jared did have an excuse, a reason of sorts, for his outrageous behavior that first night! Though probably in all innocence, Frank had, through his extravagant praise of her, whetted Jared's interest, both intellectual and physical. Nacia raked her memory of their initial meeting, trying to remember if she had unwittingly added fuel to the flame Frank had ignited.

"Come on, Nacia." Jared's coaxing voice shattered her concentration on her nagging self-doubt.

"It's no big deal. Frank meant no harm." His smile was every bit as coaxing as his voice. "I'm ready for a coffee break." Releasing his hold, he dropped an arm around her shoulders. Drawing her along beside him, he headed for the kitchen.

Instead of returning the way they had come, Jared went through the archway into the dining room, where Nacia barely had time to take in the richness of the oval cherry wood table, chairs, hutch and sideboard before he was urging her up three steps and through a doorway that led back into the kitchen.

"I like your house, Jared," Nacia complimented him as she filled the glass pot to the coffeemaker.

"Thank you." Jared paused indecisively, then added, "I built it."

"You—" Nacia's glance swept the room. "You mean you designed it?"

"No." His tone still devoid of inflection, his gaze tracked hers. "I mean I built it."

"All by yourself?" Nacia's eyes, sharper now, circled the area.

"All by myself," he concurred dryly. "It took me three years to complete."

Nacia wasn't surprised; she was stunned. Even the most ignorant observer could not help but note the care and expertise that had gone into erecting the structure. All the admiration and respect she would naturally feel for anyone capable of this kind of achievement colored her tone with awe.

"But that's fantastic!"

"Not really." Jared's shrug dismissed any claim to anything exceptional about his effort. "It's what I do for a living."

As she had spent the previous week alternately wondering what his occupation was and trying to convince herself she didn't care, Nacia pounced on his casually tossed statement.

"It is? You're an architect?"

"Nothing so grand," he drawled. "I merely follow specifications and put 'em up." He arched one brow at her. "Isn't that coffee ready yet?"

The abrupt change in the subject startled her. She was standing in front of the coffeemaker, blocking his view, and at his verbal nudge she spun around.

"I...oh...yes it is." Nacia hated the flustered sound of her voice, hated the very idea that Jared—or any man—could unnerve her without even intending to. It was downright demoralizing!

An enigmatic smile playing on his lips, Jared took two cups from the cabinet and handed them to her. "Come, join me in a cup, and I'll answer any questions you may have buzzing around in that lovely head of yours."

Nacia longed to inform him of her total disinterest in his life. She also knew she wouldn't, simply because it would be a blatant lie. She'd been lying to herself for a week; extending the falsehood to him was beyond her at this point.

With a meekness that would have floored anyone who knew her, she followed him to the table, accepted the cup of steaming brew he offered her, then sat staring into it as if expecting a tiny voice to float up with the steam and tell her where to begin.

"No questions after all?"

Absorbed with the task of forming the priority of her queries, Nacia missed the edge in his tone. Glancing up, she smiled distractedly.

"No more than a thousand," she promised, then stared in wonder at the relieved sigh that whispered through his parted lips.

Settling comfortably into his chair, Jared lit a long, filter-tipped cigarette, exhaled a small cloud of blue-gray smoke, then, an indulgent smile on his lips, gazed steadily into her eyes.

"Fire away, we have all the time in the world."

"How did your wife die?" God! Nacia could have bitten her tongue at her bluntness. Serve her right if he refused to answer, she derided herself. He didn't.

"Having our baby," he replied starkly. At her obvious surprise, he went on, "Everything had gone beautifully. Linda had a relatively short labor, and a normal delivery. Two days later she was dead from a blood clot." He shook his head as if still not quite able to believe what had happened. "The doctor explained that though it was rare—one out of thousands of births—occasionally a clot broke free to travel to the heart or lungs. At the time, explanations meant little." He smiled sadly at the memory. "She was so young. We both were."

"You loved her very much?" Nacia had to force the question from her emotion-clogged throat, not even sure she wanted to hear the answer.

"Yes, I loved her." Jared's eyes had an opaque, faraway look. "She was perfect for the man I was then."

His wording confused her. "The man you were then," she repeated, frowning. "I don't understand. Were you so very different?"

"Of course." Jared's smile was easy now. "Time and circumstances change us all. I lost a sweet, pliant, passive bride. I was left with an infant I hadn't the vaguest idea what to do with." He shrugged. "Instant maturity. Even with the help of Linda's doting parents, the responsibility seemed enormous." Jared laughed self-deprecatingly. "As you know." Again a shrug rippled over his shoulders. "Now, almost seventeen years later, a sweet, pliant, passive woman would bore me to distraction." The devil gleam Nacia had seen earlier laughed at her out of his eyes. "At my advanced age I need the stimulation of an acid-tongued, steely natured aggressor in my bed."

"You are as delicate as a moose in army boots," Nacia accused him scathingly.

The sound of Jared's laughter filled the room, and the deepest corners of Nacia's heart.

I love this man!

The realization struck without warning, scaring her, and for some reason adding to the tinge of guilt that she felt.

As had happened earlier in the living room, Jared's voice drew her attention away from introspection. "I think it's safe to say neither one of us suffers from an overabundance of delicacy." His eyes glittered with amusement. "Let's be kind to ourselves and claim forthright honesty."

There was no holding back the smile that crept to her lips. For some strange, inexplicable reason this man possessed the ability to tap into her emotional and physical responses. Nacia didn't like it, but there it was.

He also had the ability to throw her off base with his abrupt change in topics, as he proved once more while refilling the cups.

"Do you want something sweet with this?"

"I *want* something sweet with everything," Nacia responded dryly, "preferably chocolate."

Jared's lips twitched with amused understanding. "You have a sweet tooth?"

"No." She shook her head, causing the auburn waves to ripple around her face and shoulders. "Not just a sweet tooth." Her smile was loaded with self-derision. "Every tooth in my head is sweet."

The twitch widened into a grin of commiseration. "With me it's potato chips," he confessed solemnly.

Nacia and Jared stared at each other in silence for several seconds, their expressions as serious as two teenagers who had just revealed their deepest secrets to each other; then the room rang with their mutual burst of laughter.

"You know," Jared managed around the chuckle that still vibrated in his throat. "If anyone saw us now, they'd be convinced we were candidates for the funny farm."

Suddenly, inexplicably, Nacia felt completely at ease with him.

"You know," she said with a grin, "they'd be absolutely right!"

"Bump 'em all." Jared dismissed the world at large with a careless shrug, his answering grin giving evidence of relief at the dissolution of the tension. An exaggeratedly cunning look crept into his face. "I've got a delightfully sinful idea for lunch."

"I'm almost afraid to ask," Nacia laughed.

"Instead of the salad and iced tea we agreed on at the supermarket," he said in a stage whisper, "let's have a bottle of wine, a package of chocolate stripe cookies, and a big bag of chips."

"You're totally mad!" Nacia gasped on a fresh burst of laughter.

"Yeah," Jared admitted gleefully. "But I'm fun too." One long arm snaked out to coil around her neck, drawing her close to the hard length of him. "And so are you," he added softly. "That is, when you drop that cold, boss lady facade you've erected around yourself."

"Jared, don't spoil it," Nacia half pleaded, half warned, not wanting to lose the intoxicatingly light, unfiltered glow his nonsense had instilled.

The glow must have been shining out of her normally coolly guarded eyes, for Jared stared into them as if mesmerized.

"I'm not going to spoil it," he promised softly. "You are so beautiful. So warm and loving when you step out from behind that cold front of yours. The woman you keep hidden could enslave any man." His voice dropping to a hoarse groan, Jared lowered his head. "Impossible as it seems, after the week we've had together, I still want you so badly I can taste it."

"Oh, Jared!" Suffused with a warmth unlike anything she'd ever experienced before, Nacia breathed his name with a longing that was wrenched from the deepest part of her being.

"Say that again." The plea was murmured against her cheek, the movement of his lips, the moist heat of his breath a beguiling inducement. "Say my name exactly like that again." The arm around her neck tightened, drawing her fully against him. His free hand slid over her hip and moved to the base of her spine.

"Jared." Nacia's response was more a moan than a murmur. Had she been capable of thought, she might have questioned the intensity of feeling surging through her. Surely it was not usual, this young, brand-new feeling. Although the thought was unformed, she sensed it—and for now that was enough. Every bit of what she was feeling was transmitted through her husky voice when she repeated his name.

"Jared."

"That does it!" Jared's groan was so low, she wouldn't have heard it had his lips not been against her ear. "The hell with food, let's have each other for lunch."

The precedent was set for the days that followed.

The insistent trill of a ringing telephone roused Nacia from the satiated doze she'd drifted into after they had indulged their lunchtime appetite. Jared's muttered curse as he flung himself from the comfort of the wide bed brought her fully awake.

Eyes still heavy-lidded with passion spent, she watched him stride, sublimely unconscious of his nakedness, through a door Nacia had assumed led into a closet.

Why would anyone keep a phone in the closet? she wondered, her brain still foggy. Curiosity overcame lethargy. Slipping out of the bed, she scooped up her robe from the room's one chair and, pulling it on, trailed after him.

The door opened into a studio workroom-cum-office that was now bathed in gold light from the late afternoon sunrays shafting through the window-wall that faced the west. Blinking in the sudden glare, Nacia's gaze skimmed over a large drafting table with a high stool in front of it before settling on Jared's au naturel form perched on the corner of a large walnut desk.

"Oh, hell, Jake. That order was supposed to be delivered yesterday," Jared was saying impatiently as she crossed the carpeted floor to stand beside him. As quiet as she was, he heard her, or sensed her presence. Before she'd come to a stop, he raised his arm and curled it around her waist. Tilting his tousled head, he slanted her a brief smile.

"Okay, Jake, calm down." Jared's smile fled before a frown of exasperation. "For God's sake, we've been doing business with this man for ten years, and this is the first time he's been late on a delivery." His dark eyes shot a glance at the ceiling, as if beseeching help.

"Cut me a break," he went on around a yawn. "This is the first real vacation I've taken in five years. I'm trying to get a little rest." This time the smile he slanted at Nacia was outrageously wicked.

"Liar." Although Nacia whispered the indictment distinctly, her soft tone did not reach the ears of the faceless Jake. Jared responded by forming a silent kiss before grinning unrepentently. In the next instant his grin was wiped away by whatever Jake said to him.

"No, tell me about it." Jared's tone was now laced with sarcasm. There was a short pause, then he exploded, his arm tightening around her waist in the process. "What do you mean, cancel the order with Smidt and place it with Markham? Markham's so crooked, when he dies they'll probably have to screw him into the ground to bury him." He shot a glance at Nacia in time to catch the smile playing over her lips, and responded by wiggling his eyebrows à la Groucho Marx. "Don't panic, Jake," he went on, his tone soothing now. "I'll call Smidt and find out what the delay is."

Jared's conversation lasted a couple of minutes longer, but Nacia had stopped listening. All her attention was centered on Jared's features, sharply etched in bronze by the long fingers of the setting sun. As had happened that first morning on the boardwalk, she had a flashing image of a fierce-looking native American.

Blinking her eyes, she dispelled the mirage, deriding herself for fantasizing like a teenager.

"Be with you in a minute." Jared's voice drew her gaze to the instrument he held in one palm. "I have to call this supplier before Jake has a cardiac arrest." Grinning like an unrepentent naughty boy, he punched a number on the tiny push-buttons set into the receiver.

"Jared Ranklin, Bob. What's the holdup on our order?"

Her eyes drifting to examine the room, Nacia tuned out the sound of his voice. The Spartan austerity of the workroom did not surprise her in the least. The starkness was merely an extension of his bedroom.

Taking in the unadorned paneled walls, the uncurtained windows, Nacia concluded that the rest of the house reflected the budding artistic talent of his daughter. The clean lines of the house itself, and these two connecting rooms, revealed the essence of the man.

The low timbre of his voice drew her gaze to his lips, and a ripple of remembered pleasure danced down her spine. The lips moved in speech, but Nacia did not hear the words, felt, instead, the movement of those lips on her skin. The ripple became a shiver. Feeling flushed and chilled at the same time, she tore her gaze from his mouth. The action was an unwise one, for her eyes were dazzled by his naked torso, gleaming gold in the afternoon sun. Transfixed by the slim beauty of his form, she didn't notice that he'd hung up the phone.

"You're hungry again too?"

For a moment the full meaning of the question eluded Nacia, lost as she was in the warmth his husky growl sent rushing through her veins. When the context of his query registered, the warmth spread to tinge her cheeks.

"You're insatiable," she accused breathlessly.

"Greedy, too," he teased, his arm tightening to draw her to him.

"Jared, stop!" Even as she made the token protest, her fingers slid into his frost-tipped curls. "I really am hungry."

His free hand separated the front of her robe, and in exactly the same way he had on the beach the day they'd met, he laid his palm between her breasts.

"I am, too," Jared assured her in a tone gone softly, deadly serious. "And, strangely, I grow hungrier with each successive appeasement of my appetite.'' His hand moved to capture one excitement-tautened breast, and leaning to her, he touched his tongue to her skin.

Nacia couldn't utter a word. But then, she didn't have to; the shudder that shook her body told him everything he needed to know.

Nacia did not know this woman who arched herself so eagerly to his hungry mouth. She did not understand the overriding need consuming everything in its path. Common sense, independence, cold hard logic were all reduced to ashes in the blaze of desire roaring out of control in her most basic, elemental self.

There was no thought given to self-recrimination— that would come later. For now, and as long as she was near him, her reasoning power was blanketed by a fog of sensuality.

Although the belt of her robe was still securely tied, Jared pushed the material to either side of her with his restless, searching hands, exposing the ripe fullness of her body to the rays of the setting sun.

With his arm now supporting her at the waist, Nacia's body curved like a taut, quivering bow, inviting his exploration.

Head flung back, eyes closed, mindless to everything but the pleasure he could induce with just one hand, Nacia was unaware of his intense blue eyes observing her reaction to every caress, or the tender yet satisfied smile tugging at Jared's lips.

His smoky blue gaze paused a moment on her tangled auburn mane, set ablaze from the spearing shafts of sunlight, before drifting lovingly over her facial features. His eyes growing darker by the second, he made a minute inspection of her, his hand making a tactile confirmation of the satiny quality of her skin.

Very soon touching was not enough. His head moving as if drawn by a magnet, Jared placed his lips against the silky surface.

The moist, swirling pattern his tongue was drawing on her midsection drained the last of Nacia's strength. In a pose of complete abandonment she gave herself to his delicious brand of torture. A moan of shivering delight whispered through her parted lips when his teeth closed in gentle savagery on the aroused tip of one breast.

Her moan was echoed by the intrusive ringing of the phone.

"Not now!" Jared's groan was part protest, part plea.

The phone continued its shrill summons, unaffected by their human needs.

"You'd better answer," Nacia advised, gasping as his tongue traced the area recently visited by his teeth. "Jared—oh!" The exclamation was drawn from her by the sucking action of his lips.

Still the ringing persisted in its demand for notice.

"Oh, hell!" Jared growled, releasing her with obvious reluctance. Away from the tantalizing lure of her flesh, he moved decisively, if somewhat violently. Snatching up the receiver, he clamped it to his ear.

"What?" he barked into the plastic mouthpiece.

Even though Nacia frowned in censure at his tone, she understood the reason for it. Wasn't she feeling the same galling frustration? She was. She was also feeling a distinct chill, not only from the sudden withdrawal of his passion-heated body, but from the artificially cooled air in the room. Seeking his warmth, she moved closer to him, sighing softly as he rose to his feet and pulled her into a one-armed embrace. Her ear to his chest, she felt as well as heard his conversation.

"Yes, Jake," he sighed impatiently. "Yes, I called Smidt. He said the holdup was with *his* supplier. You know, it's the same story with everything these days—wheels within wheels." Jared shrugged fatalistically. "He said he should be able to deliver our order by Thursday at the latest."

Jared was quiet for long moments. Snuggled against him, Nacia could feel the tension tightening the muscles in the arm that clamped her to him. She was not caught unawares when his patience snapped; she was expecting it.

"Tell your troubles to Moses, Jake," he advised sarcastically. "*I* know this delay is going to play hell with our schedule. There is simply not a damn thing I can do about it." Again he was quiet for some time; then he sighed again. "Okay. I'll come down on Thursday and personally supervise the unloading of the order to ensure it's complete. On one condition." His tone sent a soft warning over the wire. "You hold the fort until Thursday." An oddly gentle smile tilted the corners of his mouth.

"No deal," he laughed. "You've already had two vacations this year." Without a goodbye, and still laughing, he dropped the receiver onto its cradle.

It was too much, even for the usually self-contained Nacia. Curiosity triumphing over reticence, she lifted her head from its resting place on his chest and raised her brows in question.

"Jake's my brother," he supplied after correctly reading her expression. "And he very effectively shattered the mood with his inopportune call—right?"

"I'm afraid so." Gone was the breathlessness of moments ago. Although her tone was tinged with amusement, it was definitely back to normal. "And now I'm no longer hungry, I'm starving."

"And curious about those calls," he chided.

"That, too." Shrugging out of his arms, she drew the edges of her robe together. "But first things first," she cautioned as he opened his mouth to comply. "And the first thing I want is a shower. Then dinner. Then talk."

Jared went through his Marx eyebrow-wiggling routine again. "We could save time by sharing the shower," he suggested with a leer.

Surprising herself more than him, Nacia leered back and agreed to his suggestion.

Finally, after a prolonged and very sloppy shower, Nacia, displaying an agility she hadn't been aware of possessing, eluded Jared's tormenting hands long enough to step into a pair of denim shorts and pull on a loose T-shirt.

"You're a satyr," she panted, laughing as she escaped out of the bedroom and went padding barefoot down the stairs. Jared's muttered curse against the difficulty of tugging cutoff jeans over still-damp thighs only increased her laughter.

Two thick steaks had taken temporary residence under the broiler coil and Nacia was tearing lettuce for a salad when Jared sauntered into the kitchen looking more appetizing than the meal in progress in nothing more than cutoffs.

"What kept you?" Nacia ran an arched glance over his state of undress.

"I cleaned up the bathroom for you," he intoned in pious injury.

"For me?" she yelped. "You're the yo-yo that messed it up. Not to mention the unimportant little fact that it's your bathroom."

"As you say, unimportant." Jared dismissed her mini tirade with a wave of his hand. "Now, what can I do to help with dinner?"

"Set the table, toss two potatoes into the microwave, and open the wine," Nacia instructed, fighting the smile that teased her lips.

"And what are you going to be doing in the meanwhile?" he protested.

Nacia favored him with a superior smile. "Preparing my world-famous secret salad dressing."

"Is it good?" Jared asked with mock skepticism.

"Would it be world-famous if it wasn't?" she retorted. "And, unless you prefer leathery steak, you'd better get a move on."

"Gotcha."

Forty-five minutes later, replete with delicious food and mellow with good wine, Jared helped Nacia clear the table and load the dishwasher. Then, carrying a pot of freshly brewed coffee in one hand and a bottle of Grand Marnier in the other, he followed her into the dimly lighted living room.

Alternately sipping from his cup and glass, Jared stretched his legs out before him and grinned lazily. "You have questions?" he invited in a teasing drawl.

"You said the man on the phone was your brother?" Nacia took him up on his invitation at once.

"Hmm," Jared nodded. "Younger brother. He's still a kid." His grin widened. "He's only thirty-four."

Knowing full well he was cognizant of her own age, Nacia acknowledged his implied compliment with a smile.

"We're partners in business," he went on seriously. "I build houses, Jake sells them."

"You *are* an architect!" she accused, an image of his drawing board flashing into her mind.

"No, I'm not," he denied. "I told you I don't design houses. I build them to the designers' specifications. Although—" his eyes surveyed the comfortable room "—I did some of the design on this one."

Before Nacia could comment, Jared clarified an earlier statement.

"Jake and I are real estate developers. The homes in the section we're developing now are selling faster than we can put them up. As you could tell from my side of the phone conversation, this delay in roofing materials is doing a number on Jake's nerves."

"And it doesn't bother you?" Nacia frowned, not liking the idea of Jared being irresponsible.

"Of course it bothers me." He sounded annoyed at her for having the idea. "We have a reputation for finishing on schedule. But I can't see the point in falling apart over events I have no control over." His navy blue gaze was rock steady on hers. "I may be a lot of things, lady love, but a fool isn't one of them."

"And you built this place with your crew?" Nacia sidestepped her own stupidity.

"No." Jared's smile forgave her. "I built this place with my own hands."

"But—"

"That's why it took me three years to complete it." He hesitated, frowning, then shook his head. "That's not quite true. I had started working on the house soon after Linda became pregnant. When she died I . . ." His voice trailed off and his gaze was no longer focused on her. His face revealed remembered pain—a pain Nacia now felt as deeply as he did.

"Jared, please, it's not necessary."

"I love you."

Wide-eyed, flustered by his abrupt declaration, Nacia stared at him in consternation.

"In every romantic novel I've ever read, the immediate reply to that statement was, 'I love you too.'" Jared's tone was teasingly light, but it didn't fool her for a second.

"You read romantic novels?" Nacia grabbed at the ploy with an eagerness born of panic. She had admitted her love for him to herself, but confessing it to him here, now, was beyond her. Not yet, she cautioned herself. Maybe not ever. But definitely not now. Somehow she endeavored to meet his soul-piercing stare.

"Okay." Jared's sigh shattered the lengthy silence. "I won't push it—for now." Upending the small glass, he finished his momentarily forgotten liqueur. "Why shouldn't I read romantic novels?"

Nacia blinked. This man might be infuriating at times, but he certainly wasn't dull! One should have the instinct of a hunter merely to stalk his conversational trail.

"Was the question too difficult for you?" Jared's grin appreciated her confusion.

Nacia frowned. What had the question been? Oh, yes, romantic novels, of all things!

"I don't know." Nacia's frown deepened. "I mean about your reading romance novels. Most men don't, do they?"

"Darned if I know." Jared shrugged unconcernedly, his devil grin back in place. "They do if they have anything going for them upstairs." One long finger tapped his temple. "There are some pretty good writers in the field, and intentional or not, through their work they give insight into how women think and feel."

Nacia listened to him in surprise. She personally did not indulge in romantic fiction; her reading material was usually limited to sales reports and the occasional bestseller. Casting him a considering look, she studied him as his amusement mounted.

"Brought you to a full stop, did I?" he taunted softly.

"Yes," she admitted readily. "Actually you confound me."

"How so?" Jared was laughing openly at her now.

Searching for words, Nacia's hands flailed in the air. "You're full of contradictions, aren't you?"

"Not a one," he denied stoically. "I know exactly who I am, and what I want. No contradictions. No conflict." He smiled pityingly. "You're the one with the screwed-up thinking process."

Nacia's body stiffened with indignation. "Because I don't read light fiction?"

"Not at all," he countered. "Even though you could probably learn something about relationships if you did." His head moved slowly from side to side.

"No, lady love. You're thinking is confused simply because it's all one-dimensional."

"What does that mean?" she demanded, knowing yet not wanting to know.

"I'm not the resident psychology professor." His smile gentled. "You'll figure it out eventually, I hope." Without warning, he sprang to his feet. "Let's clear this stuff away." A wave of his hand indicated the coffee tray.

Over the following days they talked incessantly—when they weren't making love incessantly. Their lovemaking was more profound and in-depth than any of their discussions.

Nacia came to know the house and the wooded four acres of land it was set on almost as well as her own apartment. Hands clasped, they strolled along a narrow creek that gurgled across his property, while Jared amazed her with his knowledge of flora and fauna.

Later, while Jared was occupied with washing both their cars, she wandered off to dip her feet into the icy creek. When he suddenly materialized beside her, she started, emitting a small screech of alarm. Feeling foolish for overreacting, she naturally attacked him.

"What are you doing? Playing Indian?"

"I don't have to play," he grinned proudly. "I am one."

One auburn eyebrow arched disdainfully. "Sure you are. Is being Indian the latest in-thing?"

"Beats me." His face was blank, but his eyes were dancing. "In-thing or not, I am one." He raised one hand, palm out in the sign of peace. "Honest. At least," he modified, "partly so. My parents assured me my great-grandmother was pure Cherokee."

"Untamed savage!"

The laughing taunt, gasped at the moment he deliberately increased the tempo of his body rhythm, was just another of the teasing comments she'd begun to make about his ancestry. Grinning wickedly, Jared flayed her with his slender frame.

"And you're one very accommodating squaw." His praise was delivered roughly through a throat arched with tension, in between gulpingly strained breaths of air.

Nacia had used his admission of owning Cherokee blood to tease and torment him incessantly every time they made love. At first, Jared had cursed himself for a fool for imparting the information. Later, he had derived a great deal of enjoyment from it. In fact, acting the savage had a great deal to recommend it.

At the height of his ecstasy, absorbing the shock waves of hers, Jared felt no qualms at all in biting her deliciously moist shoulder. The nails that raked the back of his thighs were a fitting reward for his savage performance.

God! How was it possible? Lying spent, his face buried in the side of her neck, Jared silently questioned the ever-increasing beauty and intensity of each successive joining. Almost afraid to probe too deeply into the near perfection they had found together, he mentally shied away, as if examining it too closely would dissolve it, make it null and void.

Jared had never been superstitious, or even afraid of much of anything. To find himself, at age forty-one, actually scared of shattering the tenuous relationship they had entered into both dismayed and amused him at the same time.

Some tough savage you are, he chided himself, contentedly tasting the soft skin beneath his lips. More like a marshmallow, I'd say, all rough and charred on the outside, and soft and gooey on the inside.

The July weather was as hot as they were. Neither one of them took note of the weather. One day sweltered into another; Jared merely turned the air conditioner in the bedroom up to high.

Thursday afternoon, Jared dressed in jeans, a soft denim shirt, and work boots, and left to supervise the unloading of the overdue delivery of roofing supplies.

Nacia was not especially sorry to see him go as she'd wakened with a band of pain around her head and twinging cramps in her lower right side. The moment his car disappeared down the driveway, she swallowed two aspirin, made herself comfortable on a lounge chair on the flagstone patio off the dining room, and dozed off in search of surcease.

She woke to the sound of a ringing phone. By the time she'd heaved her overheated body off the lounge chair and walked inside, the ringing had stopped.

Shrugging helplessly, Nacia headed for the stairs. Hot and sticky, she sought a shower. After the heat of the sun and the warmth of the shower, the bedroom felt like the Arctic Circle. The remnants of her headache still nagging her, she slid between the sheets with a soft sigh. Jared joined her there a short time later.

Caught up in his efforts to arouse her sleepy mind and lazy body, neither one heard the sound of the car in the drive, the opening of the kitchen door, or the quick light footsteps on the stairs. The first inkling they had that they were no longer alone was the young voice that called from the other side of the bedroom door.

"Dad! I'm home. Are you in your workroom?"

"Holy jumping hell!" Jared's muttered groan coincided with the bedroom door being flung open.

"Dad!"

Chapter 9

Nacia was not sorry to see summer come to an end. The constantly high temperatures combined with energy-draining humidity had taken their toll on everyone's temperament.

Sitting on the edge of the bed, shivering in the whirl of cool air, she stared at the pale green-and-white wall in much the same manner as she had weeks before. As on that other Saturday before she'd left for Atlantic City, Nacia was alone in the apartment. Tracy was spending the Labor Day weekend with Clay.

Weariness dragging at her spirit, she rose and pulled a lightweight robe over her sheer cotton short nightgown. Fifteen minutes later, sipping at a glass of unsweetened grapefruit juice, disinterestedly observing the trickle of coffee running into a glass pot, Nacia eyed the ivory wall phone reproachfully when its ring demanded a response. Her caller was Frank, sounding disgustingly bright and energetic.

"We're having a cookout Monday," Frank informed her after the initial greetings were dutifully exchanged. "And we'd like you and Tracy to come."

"Tracy's spending the weekend with Clay and his family." Nacia had to force an easy tone in her voice. At that moment a cookout had about as much appeal as being submerged in hot water. "And I have a briefcase bulging with sales reports I want to go over before Tuesday, so..."

"Don't say no, Nacia," Frank cut in before she had a chance to do exactly that. "It'll do you good to get out, relax and enjoy yourself for a change. I know the pace you've been keeping at work the last few weeks, Nacia. When I left your office yesterday you looked about ready to fold up." He spoke in a clipped, swift cadence, allowing her no opportunity to interrupt. "Come on, Madame Sales Manager, say you'll come. I have orders from my lovely bride not to hang up this phone until you've given me a definite yes, and at the risk of being indelicate, I really must visit the bathroom."

Even though she knew Frank was very likely lying, Nacia laughed. With the expulsion of air from her lungs, she felt some of the tension ease out of her body. Perhaps Frank was right. Perhaps being around congenial people bent on having a good time was exactly what she needed. In any case, she was simply too tired to argue. She capitulated.

"Okay, Frank, I'll come." The smile that smoothed away the tense expression on her face was genuine. "What time? And what can I bring?"

"Nothing but your lovely self! This is *our* party," Frank scolded her indignantly. "The chatelaine of the manse said to tell you you can come for breakfast if you like. The rest of the horde will be storming the walls around noon."

"Sounds noisy," Nacia observed, grinning at his insanity. "Tell the keeper of the keys I appreciate the invitation to breakfast, but I'll storm with the horde. By the way, who will my fellow marauders be? Anyone I know?"

"You'll recognize most of them, I'm sure," Frank chuckled. "There'll be a few people from the office. Some of my neighbors. My brother Bud and his family. Oh, yes, Jared Ranklin and his daughter. You remember, I introduced you to Jared in A.C. in July?"

"Yes, I remember," Nacia replied weakly.

God, no! Her mind protested in sudden panic.

Staring stupidly at her trembling hands, Nacia splashed coffee into a cup and over a wide area of the counter top. She couldn't even remember the rest of her conversation with Frank. Her movements zombielike, she mopped up the spill; then, cradling the cup, she walked to the table and sank into a chair.

Jared Ranklin and his daughter. Jared Ranklin. Jared.

A shudder shook the entire length of her body.

It had been six weeks and still the memory seared her mind, every detail as vivid as if it had happened yesterday. Closing her eyes, Nacia could hear that young voice calling from the outside of the bedroom door. For probably the thousandth time, she relived the events that followed Joyce's choked outcry.

* * *

"Dad!"

Frozen with shock, Nacia had stared over Jared's shoulder at the pretty teenager. Hand clasped to her mouth, her face paling, Joyce's dark eyes reflected anguish and disbelief.

Perfectly still, shielding her nakedness with his body, Jared issued a soft command. "Joyce, turn around and leave the room. Close the door behind you."

"But, Dad!"

"Now, Joyce." Jared did not raise his voice, yet it now held the quality of steel. "We'll be down in a few minutes."

Nausea crawling up her throat, Nacia held her breath, releasing it slowly at the sound of the door closing.

The sparks of guilt that had been flicking at her conscience for the better part of two weeks flared into full blaze. How had she gotten herself into this situation? Why had she gotten herself into this situation? Her initial assessment had been correct: madness!

Nacia shuddered from the effects of embarrassment and guilt. She hated this; hated everything about this. Damn it! Vulnerability was *not* her style!

"It's not the end of the world, you know."

Nacia raised her lids to gaze into Jared's placid blue eyes. No sign of vulnerability in those cool depths.

"Nacia, don't look like that." His calm now had a ruffled edge.

"Like what?" she asked dully.

"Like a shattered piece of porcelain." The blue depths had warmed considerably. "Honey, Joyce is almost seventeen years old. She knows the facts of life. I'd venture a guess that you look worse than she does at this moment.''

"That's because you didn't see her face." Nacia stirred uncomfortably, seeing again those shock-widened dark eyes in that pale young face.

"I did see her."

Nacia blinked against the hot sting in her eyes. Oh, Lord, tears yet! She didn't want to go downstairs and face that child! "Jared, she was devastated!"

"Nacia, stop it!" Clasping her chin in a steel-fingered grip, he forced her to look directly at him. "All right, she was shocked, understandably so. I assure you this is not a regular occurrence. But she'll get over it, and accept our relationship. I can assure you of that." His grip loosened, fingers trailing caressingly over her taut features. "Honey, it'll be okay. Come on now, we have to dress. She's waiting."

"Jared, I—"

His mouth prevented the protest. There was no pressure applied. No demand made. Instead, his lips made a silent plea for her to trust him. Releasing her mouth, he slid from the bed, scooping his jeans from the floor as he stood up.

"Joyce does know I'm a man, Nacia," he said quietly, thrusting a leg into the jeans. "And at her age, I'm sure she also knows that men *and* women have certain needs and desires." A wry, understanding smile etched his lips. "She has very likely experienced them herself."

Unmoving, Nacia watched in silence as he zippered, then snapped closed his jeans before reaching for the pale blue cotton shirt. Casting her a look that she knew was meant to pry her off the bed, he slid his bare feet into well-worn, soft leather moccasins. Still she did not move. Sharp impatience succeeded where reasoning had failed.

"Haul your tush off that bed, woman!"

Jared had again not raised his voice, but as with Joyce earlier, his tone had the same effect, and Nacia was off the bed almost before the words were out of his mouth.

Nervous fingers fumbling with the button closure on her faded denim skirt, Nacia told herself to act her age. Okay, facing Joyce would prove uncomfortable and embarrassing. It had to be done; the sooner the better, she decided, pulling a sleeveless knit top over her head.

Jared was standing at the door waiting for her, his stoic expression a strong reminder of his forebearers.

Tugging a brush through her disheveled mane, Nacia was once again struck by his fierce, proud look. If this man really wanted something, he would pursue it with single-minded tenacity and endless patience. This man was a stalker!

The thought sent an eerie, foreboding shiver down her spine. Her concept of him was at variance with the latter half of the twentieth century. There were elements of his character that did not conform to the modern pace.

There he stood: immobile, silent, patient.

With sudden insight Nacia knew that if he felt it necessary, Jared would maintain that silent stance for hours, or however long it took to achieve his purpose—*whatever* that might be.

The very idea of that type of single-mindedness threatened her in some indefinable way.

Placing the brush on the gleaming surface of his long double dresser, Nacia turned to face him, her shoulders straightening purposefully. As unpalatable as the task was, she would go with him to face his daughter; then she would collect her things and go home.

They heard the murmur of voices as Jared ushered her out of the bedroom with a mocking smile and a grandiose sweep of his arm. Her look of disdain changed to one of question as she arched her brows. Jared answered with a shrug. At the sound of their descending footsteps, the murmur ceased abruptly.

There were two young women standing in the living room. Joyce, distraught and teary-eyed, was being comforted by an extremely attractive woman perhaps ten years her senior.

"I'm very sorry, Jared," the woman apologized helplessly before Jared had taken two steps into the room. "I wanted to leave at once, but Joyce—"

"It's all right, Maryann," Jared cut in, dismissing the need to explain with a gentle smile. "You drove Joyce home?"

"Yes."

During the brief exchange Nacia studied the soft-voiced Maryann. Though small, she was well endowed, with fair, faultless skin and night-dark hair. Her eyes were almost as deep a blue as Jared's. At the moment, worry shadowed her eyes and embarrassment tinged her cheeks.

"I'll go now," she continued.

"No! Wait!"

Jared laid a detaining hand on her wrist even as Joyce choked, "Don't go!" Favoring his offspring with a sardonic glance, he drew Nacia to his side with his other hand.

"At least let me introduce you three," he went on with a hint of a drawl in his voice. "Joyce, Maryann Simpson, this is Nacia Barns." In what Nacia was positive was a deliberate move, he slid his arm around her waist. "Maryann is one of Joyce's teachers, darling."

"Darling!" Joyce gasped, her eyes shifting frantically from her father to Nacia to Maryann. "But— I thought you and Maryann were going to get married!"

"Joyce!" Maryann and Jared spoke simultaneously, Maryann in a soft cry of dismay, Jared in a cautioning bark.

Appalled, Nacia went rigid. What in the world did one say at a moment like this one without sounding like the script from a bad movie? Jared saved her from a fruitless search for words by exploding.

"Dammit, Joyce! What the hell do you think—"

"Jared, please," Maryann interrupted softly. "Take a moment to calm down." Smiling sadly at Joyce, she lifted her hand to stroke the young girl's tear-damp face. "And you take a moment to mind your manners," she urged before turning to Nacia. "I'm really sorry this had to happen." The sad smile gave way to genuine warmth. "It was nice meeting you, Ms. Barns, but if you'll excuse me, I must leave now." Without another word or glance at Jared or Joyce, she picked her handbag up off an end table and walked quickly from the room.

Nacia had an overwhelming desire to weep. She didn't. Fixing Jared with a cool, steady stare, she smiled as sadly as Maryann had.

"This is between you and your daughter," she said coolly. "If you'll excuse me, I'll leave now."

Not waiting for an answer, she turned and walked slowly up the stairs.

Her facade of coolness dissolved as soon as the door was closed behind her. She was hurt, which in itself was a new, unwelcome feeling. She was angry—at both Jared and herself. She had invited trouble with her own abandoned behavior. She admitted it, but *why* hadn't he told her there was someone else?

Striding across the room, she pulled her suitcase from the closet and threw it onto the bed, flicking the locks open angrily. It had required no more than the short amount of time she'd been in her company for Nacia to conclude that Maryann was a really nice person. Dammit! Didn't they know the other woman was supposed to be keenly intelligent, fiercely independent, and cold as an icicle?

She is.

Catching her reflection in the wide dresser mirror, Nacia stared intently into her own eyes. She was the other woman.

Her case was packed and sitting on the floor and she was closing the zipper on the flight bag when Jared opened the door and strode into the room.

"Honey, Joyce would like to— What the hell are you doing?"

Her composure firmly intact, Nacia held his sharpening gaze calmly. "It's obvious." Giving a final tug on the zipper, she set the bag on the floor beside her case.

"But—why?" Jared shook his head as if trying to clear it. "I've talked to Joyce. She wants to meet you. I mean *really* meet you." A coaxing smile played at his lips. "The worst is over, love. Come along now, please. Get acquainted with my daughter. I think you just might like each other."

"I'm sure you're right, but—" Nacia moved her head slowly from side to side. "I'm going home, Jared." She turned, reaching for her case, but before her hand touched the handle, Jared had crossed the room, his hard fingers circling her wrist.

"Nacia, I don't understand this. What are..." He hesitated, his fingers tightening on her wrists. "Is it this business about Maryann?" Jared didn't pause to let her answer. "Sweetheart, that was just Joyce's wishful thinking. Maryann is a lovely young woman, but I give you my word that there has never been anything between us."

He was telling the truth; the evidence of it blazed out of his direct stare. Nacia felt a measure of relief, but her decision remained firm.

"I'm thankful for that, at least." A self-deprecatory smile edged her determinedly set lips. "I didn't particularly relish the role of 'the other woman'—it's so very clichéd." Her gaze dropped pointedly to his clenched fingers. "Let me go, Jared. My mind is made up. I'm going home."

Raising her eyes, she caught the tail end of the expression that passed briefly over his face before his features locked into blankness. Distracted by her own churning emotions, Nacia was not up to the chore of discerning his in any depth. Had she really seen pain there? Disappointment? Frustration?

She didn't know, and at that moment she was too consumed with the need to be alone to delve into it.

Releasing his grip on her, Jared stepped back; the remoteness in his eyes was chilling. "I can't force you to stay." He smiled cynically. "I've talked myself into a box in that respect. But you could at least wait until morning to leave."

Nacia's smile mirrored his cynicism. "Why do I have this feeling of *déjà vu?*" she wondered aloud dryly.

"What are you trying to do?" Jared's tone showed evidence of the strain on his control.

"I'm not *trying* to do anything— I'm doing it." Bending, she hoisted the suitcase with one hand and slipped the flight bag strap over her shoulder with the other hand.

With a muttered curse, Jared relieved her of the burden before she'd fully straightened. "You are the most obstinate woman I've ever met," he growled, anger crashing through his restraint. "Why are you going? Can you give me one good reason for this sudden urgency of yours?"

"Yes! I could give you several!" Beginning to feel cornered, Nacia lashed out at him. "This situation with your daughter for one. I can't help but imagine what something like this would do to Tracy."

"Nacia, there's three years' difference in their—"

"But I'd be lying if I said that's the most important reason," she went on harshly as if he hadn't spoken.

"This—" She waved her hand as if trying to pluck the right word out of thin air. "This whole relationship has been wrong from the beginning."

"Wrong?" Jared's narrowing lids failed to conceal the anger flaring in his eyes. "Wrong?" he came very close to shouting. "What the hell do you mean?"

"You at least had an excuse," Nacia shouted back. "Don't try to tell me you haven't had doubts about my motivation." That she was being less than articulate was lost to Nacia. Not to Jared, who stared at her blankly. When he made no immediate reply or denial, Nacia drew a deep, calming breath. "You don't have to say anything, Jared," she went on in a rigidly controlled, quiet tone. "I understand."

"I wish I did." Jared's head moved slowly in bafflement. "Honey, I haven't the damnedest idea what you're talking about."

"My easy capitulation," she retorted. "The operative word being 'easy.'" Swinging away from him, she crossed the room and opened the door. "Think about it." The advice was tossed over her shoulder as she walked out of the room.

"Nacia!"

She didn't stop at the odd, almost desperate sound of his voice. She didn't even pause. Descending the stairs quickly, she strode along the hall and through the swinging doors.

Joyce was sitting at the table, an untouched glass of milk sitting in front of her. At Nacia's abrupt entrance she sprang to her feet.

"I couldn't help hearing you and Dad shouting at each other," she blurted. "Was it because of me?"

On sight of the girl, Nacia had checked her head-long stride. Joyce's contrite tone, her unhappy expression, brought her to a full stop. "No." Nacia shook her head. "No, dear, we weren't shouting about you." Her soft smile vanished when Jared burst through the louvered doors. She didn't look at him; she couldn't. She was hurting—badly. She *had* to get away. Masking her feelings with cool composure, Nacia tried to reassure the girl of her place. "I'm the interloper here, not you. I'm— I'm sorry your homecoming was ruined."

"Nacia!" Jared's growl overshadowed his daughter's exclamation of, "Please, don't go...."

Nacia wasn't listening to either Ranklin. Moving swiftly, she left the house. Jared was on her heels in seconds.

"Will you slow down?" His tone revealed that he was very near the end of his tether. "What is all this about?"

"I told you to think about it," she snapped.

"I'd be happy to," Jared snapped back, "if I had some idea exactly what it is I'm supposed to think about."

"Your easy conquest." Stopping alongside her car, Nacia dug her keys from her purse, then looked him squarely in the eyes. "Or are all your conquests that easy?"

"I don't believe this!" Jared's laughter had nothing to do with humor. "I absolutely do not believe this. I'm beginning to suspect your wrappings are coming loose." Reacting unconsciously to her hand motion at the trunk she'd just opened, he tossed her cases inside, then slammed the lid shut.

"Nacia, honey." His tone was pleading now. "Will you please explain what has you so bent out of shape?"

"No." Nacia slid behind the wheel. "You'll work it out."

"Oh, hell!" Jared raked a hand through his crisp curls. "I'll follow you in my car. We'll talk at your place."

"No." She turned the key in the ignition.

"Then call me when you get home."

"No." She slid the gearshift into reverse.

"Nacia." The low, warning edge to his voice kept her foot hovering over the gas pedal. "I'll call you tomorrow."

"Goodbye, Jared." Her foot pressed lightly and the car backed away from him. Swinging the wheel, she turned the car around, then drove slowly down the long driveway. Not once did she look back or even glance in the rearview mirror.

"Hey, Mom!"

Tracy's call was followed by the resounding slam of the door.

Blinking, Nacia stared at the coffee cup cradled in her hands. How long had she been sitting there, tormenting herself?

"Mother! Are you here?"

"I'm in the kitchen." Frowning, Nacia glanced around at the wall clock. Good heavens! She'd been woolgathering for over an hour. What was Tracy doing home?

"I had a blowout in my swim suit. I came home to get my other one." Tracy strolled into the kitchen with Clay right behind her.

At first sight of Nacia, Tracy's bantering tone changed to concern. "What's the matter? Aren't you feeling well?"

"I'm fine, Tracy," Nacia assured her soothingly. "Just a little tired."

Tracy was obviously unconvinced. "You've been tired for weeks now, Mom." Her eyes probed her mother's drawn face, and her state of undress. "Are you going through a change of life or something?"

"You're mother's too young for that, Trace." Clay, his own glance probing, answered before Nacia could. "She works too hard." A small smile flirted with his lips. "She always has."

"Oh, the price one pays for success," Nacia drawled dryly. Strangely, of late, Clay's presence didn't bother her one way or the other. She no longer felt the need to slice him apart with a razor-sharp tongue. Arching one brow, she shifted her glance to Tracy. "How does one get a blowout in a swim suit?"

"By splitting the rear end." Tracy grinned. "I think I'm finally getting a figure." To the amusement of both her parents, she ran her palms over her slender hips. "What do you think, Dad?"

"I think you're getting too big for your pants," Clay chided. "And I don't mean the size of your figure." With a swing of his arm he administered a light smack to her derriere. "Go get your suit, Miss America."

Giggling, Tracy danced out of reach, only then pausing to retort, "Parents can be such a drag!"

"Will you have a cup of coffee, Clay?" Self-absorbed, Nacia gave no thought to the about-face in her attitude to Clay.

For his part, Clay was too relieved to question the cessation of hostilities. "Yes, thank you." Accepting the cup, he ran an encompassing glance over her. "You do look a little tired," he opined softly. "More than a little. Are you feeling okay, Nacia?"

Refilling her own cup, Nacia paused to sigh with exasperation. "Yes, of course." Impatience underlined her assurance. "It has been a very long, very busy summer." Seating herself across the table from him, she smiled wryly. "The economic situation has everyone scrambling now. We've been chasing down every hint of a sale. I've wined and dined more prospective clients in the last few weeks than at any other time since I've been with the company." Her wry smile became self-mocking. "Hard times make prostitutes of us all."

Clay's eyes widened with surprise. "I've heard that exact tone of bitterness aimed at me," he murmured, "but never in regard to your work. You *are* tired." His alert gaze skimmed over her again. "And not only from the increased demands of business, I'd judge."

Everything in Nacia went still. When had Clay become so perceptive? When it became apparent she would not respond, he lowered his gaze to the coffee he'd been absently stirring.

Her own awareness heightened, Nacia studied her former husband. Except for the natural crinkles and creases left by time's passage across his face, Clay looked much the same as he had fifteen years ago. But he had changed dramatically, and now Nacia wondered why she had not noticed that change before.

In many ways the man she had married had been a boy. This Clay sitting opposite her was a man. A man, moreover, who by looking at her, listening to her, had discerned that what was eating her alive from the inside out had very little to do with the pressures of her work.

Though she remained still, Nacia writhed inside. Silently she cursed Jared for opening her eyes. She didn't *want* this awareness of the change in Clay. She didn't *want* this new sensitivity to other people. But momentary reprieve from her discomfort came in the form of the voice of an amazingly well-adjusted four-teen-year-old.

"Ready to go, Dad?"

"You bet, honey." Tilting his cup, he drained the last of the brew. As he stood up, he fixed Nacia with a soft gaze. "Get some rest," he advised her, then added carefully, "if there's anything I can do. . ." He let the offer trail off, knowing he was the last person she'd go to for anything.

"There isn't." Nacia confirmed his assessment. Hesitating with an uncertainty that was new to her, she sighed, then smiled. "But thanks anyway."

Clay took the smile as intended. Smiling in return, he draped an arm around Tracy's shoulders. "C'mon, Trace. Let's get out of here, give your mother some peace and quiet."

Tracy, never slow on the uptake, shifted her gaze from Clay to Nacia, a satisfied smile spreading across her face. Realizing the parental war was at last over, she exhaled a heartfelt sigh. "Right." Beaming her relief, she leaned forward to give Nacia a quick hug. "See you Tuesday, Mom." Her face lost some of its glow to the beginning of a frown. "You will rest?"

"Yes, dear, I will rest." Nacia arched one brow sardonically. "But only if you stop *talking* about leaving and *do* it."

After Clay and Tracy's departure Nacia wandered back into the kitchen, uncomfortably aware of the silence pressing in on her. Refilling her cup with the last of the coffee, she carried it back to the table, only to ignore it as it cooled to an unpalatable muddy color. Telling herself she really should get to work on the sales reports she'd brought home, she sat slumped in the chair, staring into space.

Jared had waited to call her until the day after she'd left his house so precipitately. Having slept badly, Nacia had glared at the phone when it's jangling cry woke her around eight-thirty. Barely conscious, she'd snatched up the receiver and grated a hoarse, "Hello."

"I woke you." Jared's tone conveyed regret. "I'm sorry."

What for? That you woke me or that I was still asleep? Nacia didn't voice the question. Fully alert from the instant she'd heard his voice, she steeled herself for the verbal confrontation she knew was coming.

"Did you sleep well?"

"Yes," Nacia lied blandly. "Very well."

"I didn't," Jared grunted. "As a matter of fact, I hardly slept at all." He paused, but when she didn't respond, he continued, "I couldn't sleep for trying to figure out exactly where you're coming from." He paused again, but she still refused to nibble at the bait. "I finally decided you got bogged down plowing through the desert of guilt." Nacia's low gasp seemed to satisfy him, for he went on urgently, "Nacia, we've got to talk this out."

"I don't want to talk it out," Nacia replied grimly. "It's my problem, and I—"

"What problem?" Jared interrupted impatiently. "Nacia, the only *problem* is your mind. There is no reason for you to—"

"*I* think there is a very good reason." Nacia's sharp tone sliced through his argument. "And can you honestly tell me you haven't wondered about, questioned, my token resistance that first night?"

"I don't indulge in these little exercises in pointlessness," Jared retorted. "What would it prove? What's done is done. You go on from there."

Go on? Nacia shivered. Go on to what? To where? There it was; the shadow lying over and intensifying the guilt and shame eating at her conscience.

She had failed miserably in her one and only relationship with a man, and the scars from her former marriage went deep. The experience had been shattering. The fight back to a healthy ego, an acceptable self-image, had been a mammoth task. She would not, could not go through that particular type of trauma again.

"Nacia! Are you still there?"

Nacia dismissed the fanciful notion that she heard near panic in his tone. Anger? Very likely. Panic? Forget it!

"Yes, Jared, I'm here." Nacia's sigh conveyed a wealth of regret. Her tone revealed a fourteen-year fight for self-possession. "But, as there is nothing more to say, I'm going to hang up now."

"You're going to end it just like that?" His voice was ragged with disbelief.

"Just like that," she confirmed with hard-won steadiness.

"I told you I love you. Doesn't that mean anything?"

Nacia closed her eyes in a bid to deny the pain inflicted by his hoarse, pleading tone as well as his words.

"It means you're at a susceptible age." Without conscious thought she deflected the hurt back at him. "But don't worry, love isn't terminal. You'll survive." Even as the cool assurance left her lips, Nacia winced at the cruelty contained within it. The hot sting of tears surged against her tightly closed eyelids. She had spoken to him in much the same manner as she spoke to Clay. How did one go about learning how not to be a bitch?

"God—damn—you."

Jared's grittily voiced, distinctly spaced curse was immediately followed by the buzz of the dial tone; he'd hung up on her.

"Jared."

The whisper was an anguished cry torn from her soul. This was bad, much worse than she'd anticipated. The agony she'd suffered at Clay's hands paled into insignificance in comparison to that she'd just inflicted on herself. But it had to be done.

Repeating the phrase like a litany, Nacia had cradled the sweat-dampened receiver, then curled into a ball on the bed, hot tears running freely down her face.

The phone call, though as fresh as a moment ago in her mind, had occurred six weeks ago yesterday. Nacia had questioned her own sanity throughout every day of those six weeks.

It had to be done.

Why? Drifting wraithlike through the apartment, Nacia, for what had to be the thousandth time, taxed her intelligence for reasons. And also for the thousandth time, her intellect enumerated each and every one.

First and foremost was the unaccustomed weight of shame and guilt that had begun pressing on her conscience since the moment the glow of physical satisfaction had worn off and she'd realized how effortlessly Jared had achieved his goal. She longed to relieve her mind by casting the blame solely on his shoulders, but in all honesty she could not. Had she fought him, *really* fought him, would he have come to his senses before it was too late? The thought tormented Nacia because now neither of them would ever know the answer. What tormented her even more was the niggling suspicion that he would have backed off had she really resisted him.

Compounding the initial guilt was the shame of her behavior the following morning; *she* had seduced *him!*

Whatever had gotten into her?

A wry smile flirted with her lips as the obvious answer sprang to mind. Then, with a shake of her head, she pursued the original thought.

What had caused the dormant volcano of physical desire to erupt? It had been ages since she'd felt even

a twinge of that kind of need. Completely turned off
by Clay's treatment of her, she had shuddered at the
very idea of ever again knowing a man's possession.
So what had triggered that sudden, urgent response?

From the distance of eight weeks she admitted to
feeling the lure of his attraction that first day on the
beach. The emotions that the touch of his hand on her
body had aroused in her were not the anger and disgust she'd labeled them, but were, in fact, all her
sleeping senses coming awake. Once wakened, her
physical needs had consumed her common sense.

It was as simple and complex as that.

Of course, there were other considerations, other
reasons she'd had to end the affair. His daughter was
one. Her daughter was another. Nacia had witnessed
the effect of their liaison on Joyce. She didn't even
want to speculate on how Tracy would react. Last, but
certainly not least, were the connotations and ramifi-
cations inherent in a liaison or affair.

Coming to a halt in the center of the living room,
Nacia slowly took stock of her surroundings. Everything she owned was of excellent quality. The apartment itself, the furnishings that decorated it, her car,
all belonged to her. In addition to the material pos-
sessions, but of equal if not greater importance, were
the intangibles: her hard-won self-sufficiency and independence.

Not needing a man to provide the staples of life,
Nacia balked at the very idea of needing a man to
sustain her emotionally.

Still drifting aimlessly, Nacia wandered into her
bedroom, a frown drawing her brows together when

her gaze came to rest on the white phone on the night-stand beside her bed.

Jared's second call had come five days after the first. Arrogantly ignoring the courtesy of preliminary greetings, he'd shot one hard-voiced question at her.

"Are you pregnant?"

His cold manner made her doubly grateful her headache and cramps of that last day at his house had been resolved late the next day with the natural cycle of her body. She replied coldly, "No."

There had been a pause, an instant of silence, and then he'd growled harshly, "Good."

Calling herself a fool, Nacia had unsuccessfully fought the tears that had rushed to her eyes at the jarring sound of his receiver being slammed onto its cradle.

He had not called again.

Call her.

At first the urge came in the form of a command, then as a request, and finally as a plea.

Call her.

At first the arm that reached for the plastic instrument of communication was steady with purposeful intent, then hesitant, and finally flattering with indecision.

The silent battle had raged inside his head all summer, ever since he'd called, stupidly hoping against hope that she was pregnant. That last call was the height of stupidity, of that he was positive. Lord, had he behaved this idiotically the first time he'd been in love? Jared couldn't remember exactly, but he had a niggling suspicion he had not. And he had been a lot younger then. Perhaps, he mused, we tend to get more foolish with the passing years.

The problem was, he didn't feel foolish; he felt desperate. How to reach her, how to break through her wall of detachment and expose the woman he knew lived behind it was the question that tormented him through that whole long summer.

Joyce had been the catalyst that had precipitated that very situation he had been trying to avoid. Nacia, finding herself in an embarrassing position, had withdrawn, physically and mentally. The physical distance in itself would have posed no problem for Jared. As summer waned, the mental distance seemed to grow insurmountable. Over the hot, sticky weeks, the cry had resounded ever louder inside his mind.

Call her.

Still he did not lift the receiver. Jared did not completely understand the nature of the battle Nacia was waging with herself. He did realize that her battle was a fierce one, that he could not help her in her struggle with her own personal demons, and that his future happiness depended on the outcome of her individual war.

The knowledge of his helplessness was frustrating. Work was his panacea. With each passing week his daily work hours increased—from ten, to twelve, to fourteen. His lean frame became leaner still, his patience became a thing of the past, and his sense of humor, always sharp, became nonexistent.

He knew his daughter was actively worried about him. He was fully aware of his brother's concern, despite the great pains he took to hide it from him. He could not reassure them. He felt no assurance.

By the middle of the sixth week, Jared was living on his nerves. He was smoking too much, sleeping too little. Seeing no one after work. Something had to give; fatalistically, he faced the realization that that something would be him.

When Frank called, Jared had agreed to attend the cookout on Labor Day simply because he didn't feel up to the argument he knew would ensue if he declined.

By the end of that week he had had it. He had given her all the time he could afford.

No, he would not call her. The medium of a thin wire was not good enough. Come Tuesday, rain or shine, hell or high water, he would break his own self-imposed strictures and go to her, using whatever was necessary to resolve whatever it was that was keeping them apart.

With the decision came understanding. Now he knew why he had not listened to the plea to call her. At the bottom line rested the fear of her final, irrevocable rejection, and his uncertainty as to his ability to cope with it.

Realization brought anger. Anger induced determination. Damn her! And damn Clay for doing this to her. And, damn it all, *he* would no longer wait meekly while she wrestled with herself.

He could live without her somehow, but he sure as hell wouldn't give her up without a fight!

Chapter 10

There are moments in life so fraught with despair, the soul cringes at the memory of them.

He had not called again.

Dropping like a lead weight onto the padded white velvet vanity bench, Nacia stared reproachfully at the plastic instrument, as if it had been the cause of her misery. Her eyes shifting with the restlessness that churned in her mind, her glance touched, skittered away from, then returned to a small, gleaming wood music box. Sentimental fool! Her fingers brushing impatiently at eyes suddenly hot and moist, Nacia tore her gaze from the beautifully crafted box. In defiant disobedience, her eyes drifted back to it again.

Why had she bought the blasted thing? In addition to being costly, the box was a constant reminder of moments best forgotten. A wry smile briefly shadowed her soft lips. She had known she had to have it the minute the pearl inlaid lid had been lifted and the tinkling strains of "Camelot" had assailed her ears and heart.

Stiff fingers nudged the lid, and the evocative tune sent her mind spiraling back to the day she'd first heard the clear notes issuing forth from the exquisite box.

It had begun with an ordinary request from Tracy, two weeks after she'd returned, tan and glowing, from Florida.

"Hey, Mom," she'd cried the minute Nacia had entered the apartment that Friday afternoon. "Terri has free passes to Dorney Park, and all we need is a way to get there. Will you drive us there on Sunday?"

Nacia, tired from overwork and from overintrospection, was inclined to say no immediately. Tracy's bright, expectant expression, and the fact that Nacia was leaving Monday for a week-long swing through several southern states with the regional salesman, glued the refusal to the tip of her tongue. Realizing ruefully that she had not been the most scintillating companion since her daughter's return home, Nacia agreed to the excursion.

Actually, she had enjoyed the outing with the two exuberant teenagers. The weather that Sunday had been perfect for a day spent out-of-doors. The sun radiated its gold light from an incredibly blue sky washed clean of all but narrow strips of transparent white clouds.

Nacia contributed little to the conversation during the drive to the amusement park on the outskirts of Allentown, simply because she felt unequal to the task of making herself heard through the nonstop chatter of the two girls and the blare of rock music vibrating the stereo speakers in the back of the car.

Naturally, on such a spectacular day, the parking lot was packed and Nacia had to inch the Regal into a narrow space on the very fringes of the facilities. The park was equally packed with humanity of all ages, sizes, shapes and colors. Long lines of people waited with surprising patience at every refreshment stand.

Undaunted by the prospect of standing long minutes in the scorching sunshine, Tracy and Terri, still babbling away, made a beeline for the first ride they came to after the long trek from the car to the park.

Nacia, immediately parched on alighting from the cool air of the car into what felt like a blast furnace, resigned herself to joining the queue at a stand advertising iced tea.

In between standing in line at the different rides, the girls danced around in other, shorter lines, displaying less patience in waiting to be served soft drinks, or popcorn, or pizza.

Calling it lunch, Nacia joined them in the pizza, a dull pain spreading through her chest at the memory of sharing a similar meal with Jared.

Why hadn't he called again?

With the two girls happily oblivious as they laughed their way through the day, Nacia observed the passing throng out of eyes cloudy with the question that had plagued her for weeks.

She would have bet every penny she had in her savings fund that Jared Ranklin would not give up anything he thought of as his without a fight. Without putting it into words, he had made it abundantly clear that he had considered Nacia his. Yet he had given her up.

His acceptance of her decision without argument just did not conform to the evaluation she'd made of his character. What had become of all the stoicism and quiet determination he'd displayed?

Sipping at her third wax-coated paper cup of weak, overly sweet tea, Nacia smiled at the sight of a toddler, squealing with delight as she bounced up and down on the back of a wooden giraffe on the twirling carousel, and she told herself she was every bit as delighted as that child that Jared had not made a fight of it.

Still . . .

"Hey, Mom! Are we going to stop for dinner on the way home?" Tracy put an end to her mental seesawing.

"Yes." Nacia relinquished her hold on supposition with a sigh of relief. "Why?"

"Because Terri and I were going to have another piece of pizza if we weren't." Tracy eyed her consideringly. "Could we have another piece anyway?"

"No." A smile came with her decree. Nacia knew well her daughter's appetite; hadn't she dubbed Tracy the bottomless pit?

The idea of the side trip came to Nacia as she crawled along in a bumper-to-bumper serpentlike line of cars headed toward the highway.

During a Monday morning coffee break early in the spring, Nacia's secretary, Bev, had enthused about the lovely and different Easter decorations she'd picked up in a charming shop she'd found quite by accident after making a wrong turn on the way home from visiting friends in the suburbs of Bethlehem.

"It's called the Christmas Barn," Bev had informed her. "And it really is a barn."

"You bought Easter decorations in a Christmas shop?" Nacia, used to Bev's air-headed ways in things not connected to her job, had arched a skeptical eyebrow.

"That's just the name of the shop!" Bev had insisted. "But it's open all year, and they have a terrific stock—things I've never seen anywhere else, and, oh, the most beautiful music box selection you could imagine."

Bev's glowing praise of the shop echoed in Nacia's head as she inched along the blacktopped road. In her enthusiasm, Bev had given the exact directions to the shop's location, and on the spur of the moment, Nacia decided to give the girls an extra treat by taking them to see the music box collection.

The Christmas Barn was indeed easy to find and, in fact, was—or had once been—a barn.

On entering the establishment they were greeted by a slim dark-haired woman who smiled charmingly and advised them to take all the time they liked, then offered them the interior with a gracious wave of her small hand.

As they walked by a counter, a tall man behind it called out, "Good afternoon, ladies. Please don't leave the store without seeing my pride and joy." With a wave of his hand he indicated a display case full of music boxes of all shapes and sizes.

Less than five minutes after entering the building, Nacia decided Bev had not overestimated the shop's uniqueness. Whoever did the buying, she mused consideringly, had a flare for the exquisite.

Of particular interest to Terri was the wide and varied selection of brilliantly colored ribbons in solids, plaids, and patterns. Tracy, on the other hand, was interested in everything her skipping glance touched upon.

Her perusal of the shop's wares completed, and having allowed Tracy the purchase of six gorgeous red silk roses and given Terri the choice of a length of ribbon, Nacia steered the ecstatic duo back to the display case and the tall gentleman waiting patiently but with obvious eagerness.

Without ado, he introduced himself as Frank, the owner—along with his spouse—of the business, then launched into a mind-boggling verbal dissertation on the history of each and every music box in stock, from the least expensive to one particularly beautiful work of art, the price of which brought a gasp to Nacia's lips.

Both girls were charmed by a rectangular, upright windowlike box that contained a replica of a butterfly, which fluttered when the mechanism was activated, and they were delighted by a hand-carved, gaily painted merry-go-round with tiny prancing horses.

Nacia admired them all, but withstood the urge to buy until the man's long fingers delicately raised the pearl inlaid lid of a small, satiny wood box, and the clear, bell-like tones of "Camelot" wafted lightly into the large, quiet room.

The tune had conjured up the fleeting fantasy of her time with Jared, and Nacia was a goner. Without a wince she had made out her check for a sum that many people would consider exorbitant but she thought most reasonable.

Now, seated at her vanity, Nacia's lashes flickered. Her vision clearing, her glance focused on the small box and her own fingers stroking the shiny, silky-textured wood.

Impulse buying. Shaking her head in wonder at her own erratic behavior, Nacia stood up abruptly and walked to the bed. She had never been subject to the urge to buy on impulse, she mused, tugging the covers into place. Yet the music box had been the second impulse purchase in as many weeks. Just the week before the excursion to Dorney Park, she had been shopping with Tracy and had succumbed to the lure of a rather outrageously priced blouse she did not need simply because it was the exact same color as Jared's eyes.

Erratic? With a long sweep of her hand Nacia smoothed the wrinkles from the forest-green bedspread. Erratic hardly seemed a strong enough adjective to describe her recent actions.

Nacia had always been a loner. Even as a schoolgirl she'd joined no clubs or organizations, nor had she participated in team sports. She'd been perfectly happy with a few close friends and her own individual pursuits.

Now, for the very first time, she questioned the wisdom of her chosen life-style. There was simply nothing for her to fall back on, no group or committee or league in which she could lose herself, if only for a few hours. She was strictly on her own. She had always preferred it that way. Why did it now suddenly depress her?

Sighing with weariness more emotional than physical, Nacia skimmed a critical glance over the neatly made bed. Her movements those of a much older woman, she slowly removed her robe, forgetting it as soon as it dropped to the floor. Then, absently, she grasped a handful of material and, yanking it free, slipped between the sheets. She was asleep within minutes, not once questioning why she had made the bed in the first place.

It was midafternoon when Nacia fought her way out of the tangle of bedclothes. Breathing heavily, perspiring, her mind chased the shadowy remnants of the dream that had disturbed her rest.

Raising a hand, she brushed at the heavy fall of hair clinging to her damp face. The nap had not refreshed her; if anything, she felt more drained than before. Sliding her clammy legs off the edge of the bed, she sat up, becoming still when her dull-eyed gaze made contact with, then clung to, the white phone.

Call him.

The impulse rocketed through her body, making her tremble with the need to hear his voice, however harsh its tone.

Oh, Jared. Oh, Jared, what have you done to me? I don't know myself anymore—and that frightens me.

The impulse burgeoned and Nacia lifted her hand to reach for the receiver. Her trembling fingers touched the cool plastic, then fell limply back into her lap.

What was she doing?

Suppressing a shudder, she stared at her lifeless-looking hands and drew deep gulps of air into her constricted lungs. She had severed the connection between herself and Jared with deliberate ruthlessness. She had been fighting a battle with her emotions and desires ever since. She had had six long weeks of constant inner conflict. Surely the siege of the senses could not last much longer!

Soon, soon, she assured her war-weary self. Soon the memories that disrupted her days and haunted her nights would fade; the longing to see his proud, beautiful face would diminish; the need to feel the protective embrace of his work-toughened arms, the strength of his long body hard and urgent against her softness would wither and die if she steadfastly refused to nourish it—wouldn't it?

Jumping up as if she'd been pinched in a particularly sensitive spot, Nacia yanked her thigh-length nightie over her head and practically ran into the bathroom.

The bracing, revitalizing effects she'd hoped to reap from the hot shower did not materialize. In fact, a melting languor stole over her, evoking other showers, and callused hands that lathered her skin with surprising gentleness.

"This is ridiculous!"

The wailing protest bounced back at her off the tiled enclosure. Had she really thought, just a week ago, that she was beginning to regain control over her rebellious emotions?

Yes, she had. The swing through the southern states with the regional salesman, Sandy Clarke, had gone exceptionally well. And so had the seminar she'd been roped into conducting when the original delegate had come down with a summer virus.

Nacia, fully expecting to be miserable throughout the entire trip, had been mildly astounded when, about the third day, she'd realized she was enjoying herself. Oh, she was working—talking herself to near hoarseness pacifying customers, cajoling new prospects—but she had always loved the work anyway, and she gloried in the challenge of keeping customers happy in the face of rising costs.

Sandy Clarke was a congenial companion and a super salesman. Working together, they were a formidable team. By the time they arrived in Atlanta for the conference, they were both sailing on a natural high.

Nacia's workshop presentation was a resounding success. At the dinner dance on the closing night of the conference, she was completely taken by surprise by being named Sales Manager of the Year.

Nacia would have been less than human had she not been euphoric with pleasure at the honor, and at the subsequent congratulations bestowed upon her.

As she made her way slowly through the spacious hotel ballroom greeting people, some of whom she had not seen in several years, and being introduced to others, Nacia had been grateful for the sudden urge to look her absolute best that had come over her while dressing.

Although she'd bought her dress in late spring, she'd never worn it. Other than Atlantic City, she'd had no occasion to wear it.

An hour into the evening, Nacia had decided the dress was probably the smartest purchase she'd ever made. Of a material so fine as to be almost weightless, and in a shade of pink that was sensuous rather than innocent, the not-quite-off-the-shoulder garment caressed her body like a summer breeze when she moved, outlining her form in a hint of enticement.

That evening she had received numerous compliments, and three propositions. The compliments she'd accepted graciously. The propositions she'd declined laughingly. The very fact that she had not donned the cloak of cold hauteur was an accurate barometer of her own personal winds of change.

Quite to the contrary, she had actually caught herself fleetingly considering accepting the proposal of one of the men—an extremely attractive, sophisticated man in his mid fifties—in the name of research, the object being to ascertain if she would respond sexually to any man with a degree of experience and charm.

She had just as swiftly rejected the idea, for even though the man was charming as well as distinctively handsome, she felt not the slightest physical response to him.

Nacia had returned from the trip tired but serene in her belief that she was finally getting over the traumatic effects of her encounter with Jared. Her serenity was shattered mere moments after she'd lugged her suitcases into the apartment.

"Hi, Mom!" Tracy had come running to meet her, arms outstretched for a welcome-home hug. "Did you have a good trip?"

"Yes, I did." Embracing the joy of her life fiercely, Nacia laughed.

"Profitable, too." In more ways than one, she assured herself. "Any calls?" Stepping back, she ran a loving perusal over her daughter; how very beautiful she was growing to be!

"A couple." Tracy's dry tone did not alert Nacia. "All from the same person." That information not only alerted her, it instilled a confusing combination of fear and hope. So much for serenity!

Being very careful to be very casual, Nacia laid her handbag aside. "Really?" She arched one delicate brow. "And who was that?"

"Grammy."

Nacia released the breath she'd been holding on a long soundless sigh. The shaft of disappointment that seared through her was frightening in its intensity. The sudden concern that there might be something wrong with her mother replaced the disappointment.

"Is there something wrong with your grand-mother?" Nacia voiced the worry even as it occurred.

"No." Tracy tore her gaze from a plastic bag with the name of an Atlanta department store emblazoned on it. "She wants me to come down this weekend. She's making a special dinner on Sunday for Grand-pop's birthday. Aunt Jean, Uncle Kevin, and their brood will be there." She smiled softly. "Gram wants the family around for Pop's big sixty-fifth."

Nacia smothered a groan that had no connection with her parents. She loved her mother and father dearly, and at any other time would have enjoyed the planned birthday celebration. But at the moment, she felt particularly vulnerable, and not up to deflecting the probing questions she knew she'd be barraged with when her sister Jean got a look at her.

Jean was the mother-hen type, with four children of her own, and was also four years Nacia's senior. She had an absolute thing about playing her big-sister role to the hilt. Though Nacia really did love her sister, there were times when Jean's maternal protectiveness bored her to distraction.

"We're going, aren't we?" Tracy's frown brought Nacia to the awareness of her prolonged silence.

"Yes, of course." Nacia smiled away Tracy's glow-ering expression. "I'll call Mother after I've had something to eat."

The weekend had been a success. The dinner was exceptional, which amazed no one at all as Nacia's mother was an exceptional cook. Her father had been happily content to merely have his entire family around him. Surprisingly, Jean had not gone into her big-sister routine.

The only problem had been solely Nacia's. After two days of observing the close relationships shared by her parents, and by her sister and brother-in-law, Nacia was left with a strange, unfamiliar feeling that her life was incomplete. She had been combatting the feeling every day of the weeks since then.

The shadowy movement of the reflection in the long mirror set into the closet door caught Nacia's attention, dispersing the memories. Observing that reflection, she grimaced in consternation.

She was fully dressed!

In itself, that fact was not at all earth shattering, but the fact was, she had no recollection of getting dressed!

Your mind's beginning to atrophy, she advised herself before she turned abruptly away from her frowning reflection in the glass. What you need is some food—and a caffeine fix!

Twenty-five minutes later, munching a grilled cheese sandwich in between satisfying sips of her favorite brew, Nacia's hopes plummeted as she listened to the weekend weather report on the kitchen radio.

The sexy-voiced DJ was assuring his listening audience of bright, sunny days right through the holiday.

Nacia had been holding out hope for the end of the world, or a monsoon, or an earthquake, or at the very least a really spectacular thunderstorm.

Nuts!

Chapter 11

Nacia was scared. For all her hopes of rain, Monday burst upon her small portion of the world in a glittering display of brilliant blue sky and gold spangled sunlight. It was enough to depress Pollyanna.

Raking her mind for a plausible excuse for not attending Frank's cookout, she nonetheless dressed with extra attention to detail. The contradiction did not register on the seething mass she called her mind.

She felt exhausted, yet she'd accomplished very little during the weekend. The sales reports she'd lugged home from the office late Friday afternoon were still enclosed inside her briefcase. The endless thoughts of Jared were still enclosed inside her head.

Why hadn't he called again?

Why should he have called again? She had walked out on him, hadn't she? Still, it would have been a little more flattering if he hadn't given up quite so quickly. But she really hadn't wanted to hear from him

again—had she? And yet, they had shared the ultimate intimacy of lovers; had it been so easy for him to
forget her? Hadn't she been working herself to a
standstill in an effort to blank the memory out of her
mind?

The questions and considerations bounced around
inside her head incessantly, causing a tremor through
her body.

In the process of applying eye makeup, her trembling fingers clutched the mascara wand too tightly.
Contemplating the bird's feet on the skin below her
lower lashes, Nacia scowled at her reflection. Brilliant, she applauded her own ineptitude. If idiocy was
music, you'd be the Boston Pops!

Leaning closer to the mirror, she dabbed at the
smear with a tissue, her hand pausing when her gaze
became tangled in the sad brown eyes in the glass.

Why don't you admit you can't stop thinking about
him because you're in love with him? Blinking, the
image shook its head in silent denial. I don't want to
be in love with him. I don't want to be in love with any
man.

The image shrank in size as Nacia jerked her head
back. What was she doing? Was she actually arguing
with her own mirrored reflection? This silliness had to
stop! Squaring her shoulders, she glared at herself as
she put the finishing touches to her makeup.

Rising from the padded vanity bench, she smoothed
nonexistent wrinkles from her white sailcloth slacks,
grimacing at the snug fit over her hips. She had gained
weight—at least five pounds in the last month. Darn!
Why couldn't she be like the classic heroine and lose
her appetite when she was unhappy? How boringly

plebeian she was, attempting to appease her emotional hunger with chocolates and rich desserts.

Sighing softly, she pulled a red-and-white striped middy shirt over her head. Shaking back her mass of auburn waves, she stepped into flat Italian leather slides, clasped a gold bangle-bracelet watch on her wrist and, scooping a red envelope bag from the vanity table, walked out of the bedroom. Compared to the weight on her mind, the weight on her body wasn't even worth worrying about. If she went on a reducing program, the weight on her frame would melt away. How did one go about reducing the weight of disruptive conjecturing?

Why hadn't Jared called again?

"Damn!" Unaware that she'd muttered the exclamation aloud, Nacia frowned at the fingernail she'd nicked on the Regal's door release. Sliding behind the wheel, she dug into her purse for an emery board—much used lately, as this was the fourth nail she'd torn within the last week. Though seemingly insignificant, the damaged nail was a true indication of her mental state.

Never before had she been prone to the little annoyances that had plagued her the last month. Nicking nails, mislaying keys, forgetting to pick up a favorite dress at the dry cleaner's, all these and more told their own tale of her distraction.

Why hadn't he called?

It was a never-ending mental merry-go-round, and there was no brass ring to latch on to. The feeling of being scared increased with every passing moment of the forty-five-minute drive to the Evenses' home. How could she face him? What could she say? How did one make small talk with a man one had shared the ultimate intimacy with?

Not being a member of the new wave of women who appeared capable of exiting one relationship to enter immediately into another, Nacia, for all her soul-searching, could find no answers.

Her forte had been cool indifference to the opposite sex while honing an incisive business mind, a fiercely independent spirit, and a rigid code of self-sufficiency. Did those qualities make her some kind of a freak?

Only if she'd left out the humanizing factor.

Which was?

The willingness to experience romantic love, with all its attendant joys and sorrows.

A chill had washed over Nacia that had nothing to do with the car's smoothly running air unit. Where had those last thoughts sprung from? Some prior knowledge she'd carefully buried deep in her subconscious mind?

Cautiously observing the sparse holiday traffic with her outward gaze, Nacia probed the murky depths of her conscience with the bright beacon of her inner eye.

Following her one and only emotionally devastating experience with a man, had she deliberately desensitized her emotions by applying layer upon layer of protective coats of arrogant pride, aloof independence and brittle militancy? Had she, in effect, been hiding behind a shell of cool composure?

Nacia shivered. Was there a different woman cowering deep inside of her? A vulnerable young woman, so badly scarred by the mutilating, humiliating rejection of her first outpourings of love that she had erected a psychological barrier against the emotion?

Nacia didn't have to grasp for answers anymore. The shell, though not yet shattered and lying in a thousand shards around her, was cracked; the opening was wide enough to admit the cold light of understanding. The only love she had allowed herself to feel had been maternal in nature; by then, Tracy had been a reality before the first protective layer had been applied.

Now she knew why Jared had not called again.

Jared had been the only man strong enough to penetrate her defenses, and the only man sensitive enough to perceive the inner person. Hadn't he told her he sought the warmth behind the cool facade?

Her shiver deepening into a shudder, Nacia blinked in an attempt to define the suddenly blurry outline of the car in the line before her.

As clearly as if she still held the receiver to her ear, she heard his voice of six weeks ago. "I told you I love you. Doesn't that mean anything?"

It had meant too much. Much more than she had been capable of dealing with at the time. She had admitted to herself that she was in love with him, yet, firmly entrenched in a position of fear, she had offered her own cruel rejection. The words "you'll survive" rang with appalling clarity in her mind.

When all her furious blinking proved fruitless, Nacia pulled the car into the first available parking space on the unfamiliar street and let the cleansing tears flow freely. She had no conception of how long she sat there sobbing out her regret, but when the flow was finally stemmed and she set about repairing her eye makeup, the barrier was gone.

Gone too was the crushing weight of guilt and shame. She knew now that her sudden response to

Jared that first night had been triggered by more than an overwhelming physical need. Oh, the need had been strong—and still was—but the driving force had been emotional in nature.

As trite and slushy as it sounded, even to herself, Nacia acknowledged that the starving woman inside the shell had fallen in love at first sight of Jared Ranklin.

"So, it seems you're human after all."

The words were murmured aloud at the brown eyes staring back at her from the compact mirror. Closing the plastic case with a snap, she slid it into her purse, then reached for the ignition key. She had to see Jared, talk to him, explain.

Frank's neat Cape Cod house was set dead center in a one-acre lot. Smooth lawns surrounded the house, bordered by precisely clipped hedges in front and carefully tended rose bushes in back.

Approaching the front of the house from where she'd had to park the car over half a block away, Nacia could hear the banter of adults, the laughter of teenagers. Following the sound, she skirted around the house and paused, her eyes searching for one out of the two dozen or so people there.

A group of boisterous teenagers was engaged in a game of volleyball at the far corner of the property. Directly to the rear of the kitchen door a group of women ranging in age from early twenties to mid fifties chatted animatedly as they thumbtacked paper coverings to four long redwood tables. Pounding an uneven beat on the macadamed area behind the garage, six men were sweatily occupied in a fast-paced game of basketball.

Jared was one of those men. Shirtless, his summer-bronzed torso gleaming in the sunlight, he moved with an incredible agility for a man forty-one years of age.

Tracing his every movement, Nacia's eyes devoured him hungrily. Incongruously, the first thought that struck her was: he needs a haircut. Longer, looser now, the frosted curls bounced on top of his head, clung wetly around his face and neck. The muscles in his chest, back, shoulders and arms, all brought into play by his furious activity, proclaimed a lean body in excellent condition. Nacia's fingers and palms tingled with the memory of caressing the taut skin that covered those rippling muscles. The lower half of his body was encased in faded jeans, the waistband low on his slim hips. His swiftly moving feet were protected by expensive running shoes.

While making her perusal of him, Nacia had deliberately bypassed his face. Observing his dancing moves, her eyes climbed the length of him, coming to a jarring halt when her gaze became ensnared in his. Despair stealing the breath from her chest, Nacia's body trembled in protest against the blankness in the hard blue eyes that raked over her insolently before he pivoted back to the action of the game.

In the brief instant he'd been turned toward her, the strain of Cherokee blood was evident in the harsh, unrelenting set of his features. The flat plains and rigid angles seemed to be transmitting a message that Nacia read as: For me, you no longer exist.

It's too late. It's too late. It's—

"Hi, Nacia." Deborah's greeting scattered the recurring thought. "When did you get here?"

With a wave of her hand in return greeting, and with a silent order to her legs to move, Nacia walked to meet her approaching hostess. "Just moments ago," she answered in a surprisingly steady voice. "I stopped to watch the game." She indicated the improvised court with a tilt of her head. "Is it NBA sanctioned?"

"Are you kidding?" Deborah laughed. "The Golden Age Club wouldn't sanction *that* bunch."

"Hey! I heard that." Panting heavily and sweating profusely, Frank called, "Time," then strolled to where the two women were standing. "Hi, Nacia," he repeated his wife's greeting. "I was beginning to think you weren't coming."

"Honestly, Frank!" Deborah snorted. "For a salesman, you sometimes display an appalling lack of tact."

"What? Me?" Frank yelped. "What did I say?"

During this exchange Nacia felt every nerve in her body tighten as Jared sauntered up to them to stand beside Frank. His expression was cool and withdrawn.

"Oh, really, Frank," Deborah chided with gentle exasperation. "Haven't you been telling me for the last month how very hard Nacia's been working?"

At this point Nacia was beginning to wonder how Deborah's mind was working. Apparently, Frank was also wondering. "Yes, but—"

"Will you look at her eyes!" Deborah sighed. Tiny little creepy crawlers, all with a thousand legs, invaded Nacia's stomach as both men stared intently at her eyes. She was asking herself what the hell Deborah was trying to do to her when that shrewd lady went on blandly, "From the puffiness around her eyes, it should be obvious, even to you, that Nacia is not long out of her bed. And *you* scold her for being late!"

Nacia's respect for Frank's wife went up several notches. On sight, Deborah had correctly identified the real reason for her swollen lids and overbright eyes. By taking Frank to task, she had effectively spiked the guns of speculation.

Maybe.

A penetrating blue stare made her less sure. Exerting her considerable willpower, Nacia drew the cloak of composure around herself. Avoiding the question in Jared's eyes, Nacia smiled at Frank. "What can I say?" Somehow she managed to execute a careless shrug. "I'm sorry I'm late. I overslept."

"I'm sorry I opened my mouth," Frank waved aside her apology; then, as if becoming aware of the man next to him, he added, "You remember Jared, don't you?"

"Yes, of course." Rather proud of the casual tone she'd achieved, Nacia turned to face Jared directly—and nearly gasped aloud at the knowing look on his face. "How are you . . . Mr. Ranklin?"

The mouth that had been causing her sleepless nights curved sardonically. "Very well, thank you." Jared's tone was as formal as a black dinner jacket. "And you . . . Ms. Barns?"

"Mr. Ranklin? Ms. Barns?" Frowning, Frank glanced from one to the other. "What the hell? This is a party, for heaven's sake! Can't you two use first names?"

Deborah's eyes rolled skyward, her expression revealing to Nacia that she'd sensed the tension between her and Jared. "Come along, obtuse one." Latching on to her thoroughly confused husband, Deborah urged him toward the gas grill at the edge of the covered patio. "I think it's time to start the hamburgers."

Casting another swift glance from Nacia to Jared, Frank allowed himself to be drawn away, complaining, "Now what did I say?"

Nacia could not hear Deborah's murmured response, but then, she wasn't trying to. What she was trying to do was maintain a measure of calm in the face of the storm signals clouding Jared's eyes.

"Have you been crying?" His softly voiced question sorely tested her composure.

"No, of course not!" Nacia was sadly aware that her exclaimed denial lacked conviction. "I forgot how to cry long ago." Up until she'd met him, her assertion could have been made with absolute truthfulness.

"You're a lousy liar, Nacia," Jared drawled chidingly. "Problems with the hated one?"

"The hated one?" Nacia stared at him blankly, thrown off-balance by the change from his who-the-hell-are-you expression at her arrival, to the note of concern underlying his drawling tone. "Are you referring to Clay?"

"He *is* the hated one, isn't he?" One dark brow arched mockingly. "Or have I taken over the number one position on your drop-dead list?"

Nacia's spirit, not exactly soaring with the zest of life to begin with, took a nosedive toward rock bottom. An unfamiliar sensation, uncomfortably akin to defeat, spread through her. She'd fully realized that talking to him, really talking to him, would not be easy. She'd even convinced herself she was prepared to face, and deal with, whatever attitude he presented to her. She had anticipated a range of emotions from antipathy to cold fury. But that he would accept rejection with drawling self-mockery—*that* was beyond her!

"Jared, please..." Nacia hesitated, searching for words; she couldn't just blurt her feelings out here, within view of all these people!

"Hey, you 76ers rejects." Frank's call made her search unnecessary. "If you want to take a dip in the pool before lunch, you'd best hop to it. We'll be ready to sit down to eat in about fifteen minutes."

There was the rustle of movement from the four remaining players as they broke off their conversation and headed to the above-ground pool at the far end of the lot near the volleyball net.

Rubbing a palm over his sweaty chest, Jared grimaced. "You'll have to excuse me, Nacia, while I go chlorinate my body." He turned away, then glanced back over his shoulder. "Do you think you could *survive* sitting at the table with me at lunch?" Not waiting for an answer, he walked off to join the other basketballers.

The tired term "touché" rose to taunt her as she stood dead still, absorbing the shock waves of pain engulfing her. He'd retaliated, and very effectively, for her own cheap shot of weeks ago. Knowing she deserved the verbal blow did not make it any easier to accept.

Nacia forced her hot-eyed stare away from the symmetry of his loose-limbed form. Coming here was a mistake. She should have waited, and arranged a meeting with Jared in private. Humbling herself before him would prove difficult, especially now that she'd had a glimpse of his bitterness, but humbling herself before him and a dozen or so other people was simply not to be considered. Nacia could only see two options open to her: she could cut and run, or slap a smile on her face and join the party. The falsely serene smile in place, Nacia walked to the laughing, chattering women to offer her assistance with the lunch preparations.

The midday meal was not only filling, it was informing. Deliberately seating herself on the redwood bench directly opposite Jared, Nacia blandly endured his mockingly arched brow before applying herself to buttering her ear of steaming hot corn. Occupied with the tricky business of removing the kernels from the cob without smearing her chin with salty butter, she let the table conversation flow over her until a question from Frank, seated at the end of the table, hooked her attention.

"How's the development coming, Jared?"

Losing the battle against raising her eyes, Nacia watched Jared wipe his mouth with a paper napkin before answering. "We'll finish on schedule."

"Great!" Frank congratulated. "But I thought you'd lost time because of a delay in shipment of some materials?"

"Made it up," Jared grunted, launching an attack on a second ear of corn.

"You and your crew worked overtime?" Frank chuckled. "I'll bet Jake cried like a baby over the overtime payroll."

"You'd lose." Obviously unconcerned about smearing his chin, Jared sank strong white teeth into the corn. "There was no overtime payroll to cry over."

"Jared! You didn't make up the time all by yourself?" Deborah gasped.

Frank supplied the answer. "Of course he did." Shaking his head, he smiled ruefully at his friend. "No wonder we saw nothing of you these last weeks. You've been working nights and weekends to catch up, haven't you?"

Jared shrugged. "A little work never hurt anyone."

"A *little* work, no," Frank mumbled, then, "and that's why Joyce isn't with you today, isn't it? You sent her to her grandparents' so she wouldn't be alone all the time."

"Your corn's getting cold, Frank." Jared's mild observation drew laughter from the table behind him.

"I think he's telling you to mind your own business, Frank," one laughing young man advised.

"The next thing you know, we'll be hearing about Jared being inducted into the millionaires' club," a small slim man in his middle forties joined the banter.

His second ear of corn finished, Jared calmly sprinkled salt onto his cheeseburger. "That was last month." His dry drawl produced another burst of laughter.

"But all by yourself, Jared?" Deborah's quiet voice had the tone of a worried mother.

"C'mon, Deb, I laid a few floors." Jared's tone was also quiet; his smile was gentle. "Nothing very earthshattering in that."

Nacia steeled herself against revealing the twinge of pain his gentle smile sent through her chest. Would she ever again be the recipient of one of those heartwrenching smiles?

A picture of indifference, she methodically ate her lunch while her mind boggled at her own obtuseness. At the beginning, had she actually titled him Neanderthal? This complex, confusing man who built houses with his own hands, had the intelligence to read beneath the surface of a romance novel, had the insight to recognize his own and others' emotional growth, possessed the sensitivity not only to cope with but to understand the needs of a maturing child he'd raised for the most part on his own, and to join in on laughter at his own expense? *This* man she had dared to call Neanderthal? Nacia shivered in the hot sun.

Except for the fact that Jared's manner with her was the kind one accorded to a casual acquaintance, Nacia enjoyed the day. There was an abundance of good food, a great deal of laughter, and an easy camaraderie that included her without question.

As she drove home through the softening effects of twilight, Nacia finally understood Jared's accusation that her existence was one-dimensional. What a confining life she'd condemned herself to in an effort to prevent emotional injury! Riding the elevator to her floor, she decided that if she weren't so pitiful, she'd be laughable.

Anticipating yet another long empty night, Nacia was in the kitchen pouring water into the coffee-maker when the doorbell rang. Frowning, she slid the glass container on to the unit's metal plate. As she walked out of the room, she sliced a glance at the clock. Eight forty-two. Now who the devil—? As she approached the door her frown deepened in consternation. She'd forgotten to engage the chain. One couldn't afford carelessness, even in a secure apartment.

"Who is it?"

"Nacia, open the door," Jared's voice filtered low but clearly through the natural wood panel.

Jared! Nacia's thinking process fragmented. She had prepared herself for the possibility of not being able to arrange a meeting with him for days, perhaps weeks. Now, suddenly here he was! Collecting herself, she set her trembling fingers to work on the deadlock, then swung the door open.

"I was beginning to think you weren't going to open the door." His voice was without inflection; his face was as free of expression as it had been throughout most of the day.

The sight of him caused an odd combination of joy and pain. Nacia's hungry eyes ate him up from his tousled head to his dusty jogging shoes.

His indolent stance was betrayed by the tightly corded muscles in his thighs. His eyes were that deep, smoky blue that telegraphed the tension riding him. His fingers were curled, the bones gleaming palely through the dark skin covering his knuckles.

"May I come in?"

May he? Nacia had to squash the urge to drag him bodily over the threshold. Afraid that if she uttered a sound she'd make an absolute ass of herself, Nacia merely stepped back, drawing the door with her.

Two long strides and he was standing very close. Usurping her guardianship of the door, he closed it quietly behind him. As he turned back to her, his eyes scanned the living room. "Are you alone?"

"Yes."

"Tracy?"

"With Clay until tomorrow."

"Good."

After their terse exchange, the silence that fell between them seemed doubly heavy. When he didn't elaborate on why he thought it good she was alone,

Nacia drew a slow, long breath and forced herself to ask, "Why?"

He shrugged. She frowned. His manner was so uncharacteristically uncertain; he confused her. She had chafed at having to wait to talk to him, yet now that he was here she didn't know where to begin.

"I . . . ah, I just made some coffee," Nacia blurted, fully aware of her own delaying tactics. "Would you like some?"

"Yes. Thank you."

Nacia would have been more than a little surprised had he refused, for during the time they'd spent together she'd come to realize he was as addicted to caffeine as she was.

Leading the way to the kitchen, Nacia berated herself for her own uncertainty. God! She had always been the least uncertain person she knew!

"Have a seat." The invitation was issued with deceptive calmness as she withdrew two earthenware mugs from the cabinet above the coffeemaker. As she placed the filled mugs on the table, Jared arched a dark brow.

"You wouldn't happen to have something to lace this with?"

"I have a bottle of brandy a customer gave me for Christmas last year. Will that do?"

Jared's lips twitched with a hint of a smile. "Admirably."

After she found the squat, round bottle in an out-of-the-way cabinet, Nacia set it close to his hand, then sat down opposite him, frowning when he poured a small measure of the amber liquid into her cup. "Am I going to need fortification?"

Once again his shoulders moved briefly in that oddly uncertain shrug by way of an answer.

Following his example, she lifted her cup and sipped tentatively at the fragrant brew. Surprisingly, it was quite good. Raising her eyes, she offered a hesitant smile. "I rather like it."

"I rather love you."

Nacia's mug landed on the table with a dull thunk. Steadying the mug with hands that felt ridiculously boneless, Nacia stared at him longingly. When, finally, she managed to push some whispered words through her lips, she amazed herself by repeating Deborah's admonition.

"All by yourself, Jared?"

Though Jared looked startled, he understood perfectly. This time his shrug conveyed mild impatience. "I said it was no big deal. Besides, it gave me something to do with my nights."

"Jared—"

"No!" He moved his hand in a silencing motion and, as if afraid she'd say something he didn't want to hear, went on tersely, "Nacia, please don't interrupt. I've spent six weeks, six long weeks, thinking about you, aching for you. I was *glad* for the extra work, simply because it kept me busy. When you told me I'd—" his mouth twisted in a swift grimace "—survive, I thought, You're damn right I will, and I have. But, God, it hurts." The harsh set of his features showed how much it had cost him to admit to feeling that hurt. "Honey, after what you told me, I understand why you've been afraid to open yourself to a man—any man. But the time we spent together was so good, it felt right." He shook his head.

"When you left the house, drove away from me, I just couldn't believe your action was final. I was convinced that after you'd thought about it, you'd realize that what we had together was worth working on, building on.

"When I called you the next day I really believed that all we had to do to make things right between us was talk it all out. Because *I* knew what we'd found together doesn't come whistling down the pike but once in anyone's lifetime. I guess I assumed you knew it too."

Nacia couldn't speak past the tightness in her throat. She had yearned for the opportunity to explain to him, yet here she sat, mutely watching him drain the coffee from his cup as if his throat were parched. It seemed the longer she remained silent, the tighter his expression became.

"Jared, please listen, I—"

"Dammit, Nacia, why can't you trust me?" The harsh intensity of his tone sent a shiver through her; he sounded very much like a man at the end of his rope. "I'm not like *him*. I won't hurt you. I'll protect you, cherish you." He shook his head defeatedly. "I don't want to own you. I don't want to rob you of your independence. I want you the way you are—the woman I knew I had to have from the moment I saw you on the beach that day. I want to laugh and fight with you during the day, and make love to you most of the night. I'm forty-one years old, Nacia. *I* know what I want."

"You never called me again."

"No. I didn't call again." He stared at her hard; then he sighed deeply. "As I said, I told myself I damn well would survive. Only a fool would go back for that kind of punishment." Lifting his right hand, he rubbed the back of it against the left side of his jaw. "I lived through pain before. When Linda died, it was bad. I cried, and the crying helped, it eased the hurt inside. I endured the finality of death. I didn't call again because I wasn't sure I could endure the finality of your rejection."

"Oh, Jared!" The tightness in her throat dissolved with the tears she allowed to run unchecked down her cheeks.

"Nacia, don't cry!" Jumping up, he came to her to grasp her arms and lift her from her chair. "Darling, stop." Raising a hand, he brought it to her face to brush at the tears with his fingertips. "You never cry, remember? You forgot how long ago."

"You were right," Nacia told him tremulously. "I lied. I seem to be crying all the time lately. Oh, Jared, I'm such a fool."

"No," he denied softly. "I'm the fool. I realized how much of a fool when I glanced up and saw you at Frank's today."

"You looked so fierce, so—so withdrawn from me." Nacia sniffed. "You scared me."

Jared smiled in self-derision. "You certainly didn't look scared. As a matter of fact, I thought *you* looked distinctly disinterested in *me*." The smile disappeared. "Even so, then and there I decided to follow you home tonight, no matter what time the party broke up." The derisive smile appeared briefly. "You know what they say about fools rushing in." His hand spread out along her jaw. "I must kiss you, darling, just once."

Bending his head, he touched his lips to hers for a gentle, sweet moment. Nacia felt a shudder go through his body; then his mouth crushed hers, his tongue spearing inside with a hungry demand he could no longer control.

Sliding her arms around his waist, Nacia clung to him, loving the hard feel of him against her. When he lifted his head, she stared into the darkness of his eyes.

"I am a fool," she whispered. "And arrogant. And proud. But most of all, I'm a coward. A coward who was afraid of life and love. I've spent the last six weeks telling myself there's no room in my life for love."

Nacia felt the flicker of pain that shadowed his face. Her throat ached with the groan that rumbled in his.

"Nacia—"

"No." She lifted her hand to cover his lips with her fingertips. "It's my turn now. You see, I decided while driving to Frank's today that I had to talk to you, try to explain the reasons for being the way I am." She frowned. "Of course, it immediately became evident I'd get no opportunity for a private conversation with you there. I was going to call you tomorrow, ask you, beg you if necessary, to meet me someplace where we could talk in private." She moistened her lips, then went on softly, "I'm still afraid, darling." Nacia liked the sound of the endearment as it whispered through her lips. "But I love you so very much I can't hide from it any longer."

"Now I must kiss you again." The teasing devil was back in his eyes, but his voice had a shaky note, somewhat like a man who'd escaped injury by a hair.

Lifting his other hand, he cupped her face. Slowly, caressingly, he kissed away her tears before covering her mouth with his. This time his kiss was different. It was a blessing. A promise. A thank-you.

"No more guilt craziness?"

"No." Nacia shook her head. "I think I fell in love with you that day on the beach. My body just realized it before my mind did."

"I know there'll be problems, honey." Jared smiled with soul-stirring tenderness. "My house. Your apartment. Our work. Our daughters. We'll work it out."

"We'll have to." Nacia was dead serious. "I don't think I could bear being separated from you for six weeks again."

This time she kissed him. He obviously loved it, for his arms dropped to close around her like a vise and his lips grew hard with need.

"Are you going to kick me out of here tonight?" Raising his head, his eyes challenged hers.

"No." She met the challenge with a kiss-softened smile.

"In that case, darling, why don't you take me to bed?"

Slipping out of his arms, grasping his hand in hers, Nacia did exactly that.

There are moments in life so serene in their passage, the risk of taking them for granted is understandable.

Crossing his ankles as he settled more comfortably in the lounger, Jared raised his glance from the newspaper he'd been reading, a smile curving his lips as his blue gaze came to rest on the woman curled into the corner of the long sofa.

It was midmorning of a Sunday in January—a morning cast into near silence by a heavy blanketing of snow. She was dressed in a long caftan, her hair a mass of auburn waves around her face. At the moment, she was totally absorbed in the book she held in one slim hand. The book was the cause of Jared's amusement. It was one of his. The cover, depicting a man and woman in a crushing embrace, proclaimed its genre of romantic fiction. It was not the first of his books that Nacia had borrowed—all in the name of research, she had hastened to assure him.

Shifting his glance, he stared, mesmerized, at the steadily falling snow; it had been coming down since early afternoon the previous day. The curve at his lips grew wider at the memory of his telephone conversation with her the morning before.

"I'm coming up," Nacia had stated flatly, not bothering to return his ritual greeting.

"I thought the plan was for me to come down?" Jared had replied blandly, unperturbed by her bluntness. "I seem to recall your mentioning the desire to see a particular movie this weekend."

"Yes, well, that was before the weather service began predicting the possibility of a heavy snowfall tonight."

"I think you lost me, love." Jared's tone held a grin. "What does the weather forecast have to do with a critically acclaimed film?"

"Not a damned thing," Nacia had retorted. "The weather forecast has to do with getting snowed in; and if we're going to be snowed in, I'd just as soon it be at your place."

"Any particular reason?" he'd inquired in a patently false innocent tone.

"One," she'd replied, matching his innocence. "Chances are slim to none of being snowed in for any appreciable amount of time here, so close to the city.

On the other hand, out in the boonies we could be confined for days.''

Dropping all pretense at confusion, Jared had laughed out loud.

The threatened storm having materialized, all indications were that they would indeed be marooned for several days. It was a delicious thought—one that sent a tingle of anticipation careening down Jared's spine.

These frequent anticipatory tingles no longer amazed him. Even after five months of spending every available minute together, the mere thought of being alone with Nacia set his pulses to hammering wildly, started his body juices cooking. The fact that they were completely alone, Joyce having gone to her grandparents' for the weekend and Tracy being with her father, was an added delight.

No longer seeing the sparkling white crystals, Jared mused over those previous five months. In effect, they had not removed any of the obstacles in the path of their being together; they had simply worked around them. She still lived in her apartment, he in his house. They both still pursued their choice of work rigorously. They argued often. Strangely, their respective daughters had accepted their liaison in stride—thereby displaying a maturity that was surprising, but gratefully acknowledged. Marriage was never mentioned.

Jared, discovering a fierce streak of possessiveness he had not realized he was capable of, longed to legalize their union, to bind her to him with every available measure. Prudently, he did not attempt to force the issue. When she was ready, he cautioned himself. Until then, he honestly admitted, he would use any means to hasten her final surrender. The contemplation of those means increased the intensity of the tingle, drawing him back to the here, and the now, and the night they had spent together.

Fully aware of the cold, white world outside, they had luxuriated in the warmth of his room, the comfort of his bed. Their bodies unhampered by constricting clothing or covers, they had teasingly, laughingly made love through the majority of the snow-swept night.

The memory fragmented the tingle at the base of his spine, sending shock waves radiating around his hips to converge with building urgency in his groin.

"Jared?"

The sound of Nacia's soft, warm voice teased the tingle into a pleasurable pain.

"Darling, what are you so deep in thought about?"

His eyes nearly black, Jared turned to face his love with a beguilingly wicked grin. Her answering grin was every bit as wicked, but there was something else there, too, something that made her eyes shimmer as if in sudden, happy expectation. That something stopped the breath in his chest, alerted every one of his senses, hummed through his still, excitement-tautened body. Jared knew, yet was afraid to know...in case he was wrong.

Nacia, bright eyes observing every nuance of Jared's expression, smiled brilliantly, and blinked furiously against the sudden hot sting of moisture in her eyes. God! She loved this man! More than herself! Possibly more than her own precious child! And she had drawn out the vibrating stillness in him long enough. Even though she swallowed and wet her lips, her voice cracked.

"Will you marry me?"

Slowly, slowly, Jared released the air in his tight chest. With the gentle smile that touched his lips, the glow that lit his eyes, and the adoring expression, words would have been redundant. His gaze almost as misty as hers, Jared lifted his arm and held his hand out to her, unashamed and uncaring of the slight tremor in his fingers.

There are moments in life so incredibly beautiful...

* * * * *